MURDER ON THE
INTERGALACTIC RAILWAY

A RITCHIE AND FITZ SCI-FI MURDER MYSTERY

KATE MACLEOD

Cover image by Benjamin Roque

Ratatoskr Press logo by Aidan Vincent Kise

ISBN 978-1-951439-02-6

❋ Created with Vellum

1

THIS, Murdina Ritchie thought, was as close as she ever expected to get to a perfect moment.

She knew the panorama arching over the crowded terminal floor was fake. The Intergalactic Transport Depot Delta-Gamma-Delta was convenient to a handful of jump points, but nowhere near anything as picturesque as the pink, lilac and blue nebula shimmering so intensely she felt like she could reach out and touch it. No, it was just an illusion to cheer the weary traveler, of which she was one of billions.

But the warm bulb in her hand was real, and she had waited four years to taste its contents again. She hadn't needed it in a bulb—her travel plans weren't going to involve any stints in free fall—but the language barrier between her and the race of creatures who sold what she knew to be the best drink in the galaxy had been sizable. Her attempts to pronounce the name of the drink had been met with puzzled blinks, but the words "uber coffee bomb", spoken by the smiling man waiting behind her in line, had triggered a fluttering of tentacles that ended with her with this bulb in her hands, minus every bit of pocket change she had been saving over the last year. She was just happy to have gotten it in any form at all.

And she still had time left to get to the correct terminal ahead of schedule to report to the officer from the Oymyakon Foreign Service Academy.

Her stomach had been a tight knot of nerves for, in retrospect, most of the last four years. And it would knot up again in just a few minutes, she was sure, in advance of the moment she would meet the officer and her new fellow cadets.

No one was going to call her by her first name anymore. It would be Ritchie, just Ritchie. All day, every day, nothing but her family name. Every time she thought of that, that constant reminder of her father, the knots would tighten even more.

But for just one moment, one last perfect moment, all her stomach felt was a rumbling longing for what it knew was in her hand.

She slipped out of the crowd of her fellow travelers—some human like her but others of a wider array of species than even she with all of her studying could name—and perched on the edge of a raised plant box where she could look up at the nebula while she sipped at her treat and not get jostled.

Once settled with the bag with her personal possessions tucked close to her side, she turned her full attention to her treat. She squeezed the bulb ever so gently so that its neck opened up enough for her to get a whiff of its rich, sugary contents. The caramel smell was just as she remembered from when she'd had this drink once before. But there was something else laced beneath it, sort of a smoky aroma, that she didn't remember at all.

It wasn't coffee, not really. She had never had coffee before her grandmother had first given her this drink four years ago, but she had had a lot of coffee since. Some good, some bad. Now that she had more of a palate, what would this taste like to her? Was she about to be disappointed?

Ritchie pushed away the thought and took a sip. The first part was all creamy foam, rich and almost too sweet. Then a splash of the hotter liquid below reached her lips, and that smoky aroma became a smoky, roasted flavor that made every cup of coffee she had ever had dull and bitter by comparison.

Ritchie let the bulb close up in her hand, looking up at the holo-gram of a nebula overhead as she let that little sip linger on her tongue as long as possible.

Even better than she remembered.

She sat with the warm bulb in her hand, watching humans and aliens pass in front of her as she spaced out those little sips as much as she could bear.

The travelers on the shuttle with her had been, by virtue of the design of the seats more than anything, entirely humanoid. Their skin and hair had been a variety of colors and textures, and many had needed breathing apparatuses over their mouths to adjust human-stan-dard environmental settings to their personal needs, but they all had walked upright on two legs and were accustomed to gravity or grav-ity-simulating spin.

But an endless variety of beings were bustling through the main terminal. She saw water-based creatures in liquid-filled suits that either simulated bipedal motion or hovered along like floating aquari-ums. She even saw a few air-based beings, traveling inside the safety of containment fields to keep themselves from dispersing, or, perhaps more importantly, to keep others from blundering into their wispy forms.

From what she had studied in school, most air-based beings weren't harmed by being disrupted like that, but she imagined it was deeply annoying. She had never met one before, although she had seen a few back home, especially when she had spent time waiting in the hall-ways of government buildings with her mother.

What a strange life it must be, to be a cloud.

Ritchie was used to moving through crowds back on the space station she called home, but the sound here was very different from the chaos of her neighborhood. It was more like in those government buildings, with many people moving together inside the confines of noise-blocking bubbles so that their conversations would not be over-heard by others. She could see the shimmering of the air around them, watch the noiseless moving of their mouth or other speaking appendages.

She knew the bubbles only suppressed the sound from within them, but she could never shake the feeling that they were sucking the sound out of the rest of the world, too. She should be hearing a lot more swishing of clothing, a lot more sniffles and coughs, a lot more scuffling of feet. But mostly what she heard was the soft whir of drones hovering over the crowd, watching for any need that might arise they could assist with, and the deeper hum of floor robots constantly tidying up after the never-ceasing throng of beings moving through the depot.

What languages she could hear were all strange to her ears. If she really focused on any one voice her implant would offer to translate for her, but she knew from experience it would remind her first that this was considered rude in most cultures.

Ritchie grinned. This was the world she had longed for, the world she just knew she belonged in. Full of... well, everything and everyone.

But where she was going, a remote academy on a remote planet, was about as far from everything else as it was possible to get.

It was only for three years, she reminded herself. Less than that, since she was starting the year late because of her delayed acceptance.

Her little self-pep talk didn't help. Her stomach was twisting in nerves again, and her happy moment had passed.

She glanced at the chronometer in the corner of her vision and decided she should probably find the meeting point, just in case it wasn't somewhere obvious. The bulb in her hand was still warm and still more than half-full, but the longing for sweet, rich delight had passed.

Hopefully, it would come back. She wasn't likely to get anything this good at the academy. She didn't want to waste a drop of what she seemed doomed to always wait years for.

Her implant offered her a map of the station, but with everyone moving around her, she was afraid it would be too disorienting to navigate that way. The last thing she needed was to get lost and miss the train. She dismissed it in favor of a little glowing light only she could see that would lead her through the throng to where she was supposed to be.

The crowd closed in around her, sweeping her along like a river of sentient beings. The light in front of her flashed at her that she had reached her destination, but at the same moment, something flared overhead. A part of the already glorious nebula erupted into a truly spectacular show of color and light.

Her guiding light flashed again, and a notification sounded that only she could hear. She tried to step to the side, out of the flow of bodies, but her eyes were still on the dome above her. She felt her foot catch on the wheel of some conveyance and looked down, but too late to avoid the thick passing tentacle that swept her other foot out from under her.

She was falling. The only instinct she had left was to raise the bulb so it wouldn't get crushed beneath her.

That might have worked, if someone else hadn't stepped forward to catch her. The hand on her left elbow was steadying, and it did indeed keep her from crashing to the floor.

But there was no matching hand on her right side, nothing to stop her shoulder from colliding with the broad chest of her rescuer.

And the bulb she had tried to thrust up out of harm's way had only made it to the level of her shoulder before that impact.

The bulb was designed to tumble through free fall without leaking. It was even designed to hit a wall or two without losing a drop.

But it wasn't designed to be violently crushed between two bodies.

"Oh, no!" Ritchie cried as the air filled with the sweet smell of caramel and the smoky undertones of whatever those aliens roasted that was not quite coffee. Her cry was one of mourning for what she had just lost. Every drop was gone, splattered all over her uniform that had still had that newly replicated smell up until just a second ago.

And all over the remarkably similar uniform of the man who was still holding her by the elbow.

"Oh, no," Ritchie said again, her mourning turning to despair.

She doubted it was possible to make a worst first impression.

"Cadet..." the dark-haired man said, looking down at the name tag on her uniform, mostly obscured by white foam now. "Ritchie, is it?"

Was there an edge to his voice when he said that name? Some hint of familiarity, of contempt? She looked up at his face, but his expression was inscrutable. All she could tell was that he was getting impatient, waiting for her to answer him.

"Yes, sir," she said miserably, but when he narrowed his eyes at her, she snapped to attention. "Sorry, sir."

"Don't apologize to me," he said sharply. He held his hands in front of his own chest, but then resisted the urge to wipe the mess off of himself, opting instead to wave a finger in the air until he had the attention of one of the hovering drones. "Sorry doesn't undo a mistake, cadet."

"Yes, sir," Ritchie said. She was spared having to find anything else to say when four drones descended on them, suctioning up every sign of the drink from both of their uniforms as well as the floor and, to her surprise, her hair. As the drones worked, she tried to sneak a few glances at the officer without him noticing.

He looked old enough to be retired, although his hair was jet black and so thick that even with its regulation short cut, no scalp showed through. But the olive-colored skin of his face bore some kind of scarring she had never seen before. Was that from some past battle, or maybe an environmental mishap?

The drone whisked away the last of the foam from the front of his uniform and she saw his name and rank. Colonel Hansen.

"Colonel Hansen," someone else said. Ritchie turned to see a petite blonde girl standing behind her, also dressed in a cadet's uniform and offering a crisp salute. The colonel returned it, then waved the still-hovering drones away. "Cadet Moreau reporting for duty," the girl said.

"At ease," the colonel said. "We're still waiting on two others."

Moreau relaxed her posture, then turned her attention from the colonel to Ritchie. Moreau's assessing gaze ended in something Ritchie was sure was a smirk. Surely the drones had cleaned up every sign of the coffee mishap. She felt her cheeks reddening and fought the urge to touch the ends of her newly cut hair. Was the style not right? Was she going to stand out?

Moreau had all of her pale blonde hair twisted into a knot on the top of her head. She was so slight of frame Ritchie wondered how she had even passed the physical requirements. Was the topknot there to add just a little bit of needed extra height? But there was no way anyone could cheat like that. She must have qualified.

"Cadet Ritchie," Moreau said, reading Ritchie's name tag. Again Ritchie found herself searching a tone of voice for clues, only this time she could feel the colonel's eyes on her, watching her as she did it.

"Cadet Moreau," Ritchie said, as if Moreau had spoken in greeting and not with that little lift at the end that just suggested a question. Or maybe a challenge.

Moreau seemed to find that amusing, but before she could speak they were joined by another young cadet, this one a boy with reddish-brown hair just starting to curl at the ends despite the shortness of its cut. He snapped to attention just behind Moreau, his hulking frame with its broad shoulders and almost excessive height completely dwarfing her.

"Cadet Weld, sir," he said to the colonel. "I'm on time?"

"Is that a question, cadet?" the colonel asked. Ritchie expected him to raise an eyebrow as he spoke, but the colonel's face didn't move at all, his expression revealing nothing. Cadet Weld was clearly forcing himself not to squirm.

"A statement, sir," he said firmly.

"And a correct one," the colonel said. "If just barely." Then he seemed to dismiss all three of them from his mind as his eyes scanned the crowds around them.

"Hi," Weld said to Moreau. She actually snorted and rolled her eyes, to Weld's obvious confusion. He looked to Ritchie, as if uncertain whether he should even try speaking to her.

"Hello," Ritchie said, thrusting out a hand for him to shake. "I'm Cadet Ritchie."

"Pleased to meet you," he said, and returned her smile. But then something else passed over his face, a look of wonder or puzzlement. "Ritchie. I know that name from somewhere. Is it common in this quadrant?"

"Not that I know of," Ritchie said. "I'm not from here myself."

"Oh," Weld said with a shrug. "Me neither. But I thought maybe I went to school with your brother or cousin or something."

"I'm an only child," Ritchie said, then added for good measure, "an only child of only children. So no brothers or cousins."

"That's a shame," Weld said.

"Is it?" Ritchie asked.

"Well, maybe not to you," he quickly amended. "I have five brothers, three sisters, and more cousins than I can count. I can't imagine not having any."

"Well, it's all I've ever known, so..." Ritchie said, ending with a shrug.

Moreau snorted again. Ritchie turned to look at her, but Weld spoke first.

"I suppose you're an only child as well," he said, and this time it was very clear that to him this was a bad thing.

"Of course," she said with a toss of her head. That gesture suggested to Ritchie that Moreau usually wore her long blonde hair down, and that it would flip in a supercilious manner when she tossed her head like that. To drive home whatever point she had just made. "But you *do* know why her name is familiar, don't you?"

"Do I?" Weld asked, looking to Ritchie.

"I think we just established that it isn't familiar," Ritchie said. She could feel the colonel's eyes on her again, and the knots in her stomach drew tighter.

Moreau knew. And she was certain that the colonel knew as well.

But Weld didn't seem to.

"How do I know the name Ritchie?" he asked.

"Gustav Ritchie," Moreau said. Then, at Weld's deepening frown, "Gustav Ritchie, the diplomat?" Weld just shrugged, and Moreau rolled her eyes even more than she had before. "The diplomat who has taken by the Yuffids five years ago and no one knows if he's alive or dead?"

"Four years ago," Ritchie said, but barely more than a whisper.

"Oh, right," Weld said. At first Ritchie thought he was lying, only pretending to remember what Moreau was referring to. But then a series of micro-expressions cascaded over his features as detail after detail of the story came back to him. Recall turned to horror and then to pity before Ritchie turned away.

It was going to be like this. Again and again and again. When she met the last cadet here, and then when she reached the academy.

And again when she went on to higher training, and got her first posting, and every subsequent posting.

She would live this moment over and over again for the rest of her life. She knew she would.

She only hoped that eventually her heart would grow some kind of emotional callus. It had to at some point.

Didn't it?

"I'm sorry," Weld said, as if he had been the one who had dredged up all the pain.

Ritchie took a deep breath and turned back to the others, but they were both looking at the colonel now.

"We've waited long enough," he said, pointing the way across the terminal. "Our train is about to leave, with or without us. I guess we'll be short one cadet, but given his record, I'm not sure it's much of a loss."

"Our airlock is that way," Moreau said as the colonel headed off in what Ritchie's implant, too, was telling her was the wrong direction.

"We'll never reach it in time," he said. "This one's closest. Step lively."

The three of them clutched their shoulder bags close and tried not to lose the colonel or each other in the crowd that seemed determined to keep flowing in the other direction. Like it didn't want them to reach the train in time.

"Stay behind me," Weld said to her and Moreau. "I'm wide enough to break a path."

"Thanks," Ritchie said, and found herself tucking close against Moreau's side. Ritchie was pretty sure she hadn't made a great first impression with any of them except maybe Weld, but there was still two days' worth of journey to turn that around before they reached the academy.

Well, she always relished a challenge.

Ritchie could see the airlock and was prepared to step inside when instead she collided with Weld's suddenly immobile back. She peaked around his arm to see the colonel standing speechless inside the airlock watching a young man in a steward's uniform trying to shoo him back out.

"Should we run?" she asked.

Moreau laughed. "Like this kid is going to tell the colonel what to do."

And indeed the colonel only waited for the young man to pause for breath before putting a hand on his shoulder and propelling him back into the train corridor, waving for Weld to step into the now-open space of the airlock.

"This isn't your car, sir!" the steward said, tugging at the hem of his uniform jacket as if that somehow lent him a measure of authority.

"It's a train, son. They all connect," the colonel said. "You're about to depart, and I don't fancy running to get to some arbitrary train car when this one will do."

"This one will not do!" the steward said huffily. "This is a VIP car."

"We'll just pass through. We're not looking to bother anybody," the colonel said reasonably. He tried to put a hand on the steward's shoulder to draw him away enough to let Weld into the corridor, but the young man twisted away from his grasp.

"Come on, hurry. I can see the indicator panel on this side and the doors are about to close," Weld said, squeezing into a corner enough to let Moreau slip past him.

Moreau, who was maybe half the size of Ritchie.

"Come on," Weld said again, pushing himself up on tiptoe as if he could tuck himself up near the ceiling. Moreau reached out as well, and Ritchie took her hands and somehow wedged herself into the airlock.

"Good thing that other one never showed up. There'd be no room for a fourth," Weld said, and Moreau gave her little snorting laugh.

But Ritchie's laugh of agreement died on her lips as she looked back out across the terminal and saw the last cadet slipping like a fish upstream through the press of bodies.

She knew that chaotic mess of brown hair. Even before his face came into view, she recognized that hair.

He burst out of the crowd, but something had caught at him

because his run had become a stumble. But he didn't fall. He caught his balance, then lifted his head and looked right at her.

She definitely hadn't forgotten those eyes. And she knew the minute they met hers, he hadn't forgotten her either. She could feel that old energy pass between them, like they shared a mind and words were unnecessary for them to understand each other. Four years apart hadn't diminished that one bit.

Shackleton Fitz IV.

Then the airlock door started to close.

2

SHACKLETON FITZ IV, who never let anyone call him anything besides just Fitz, collapsed against the airlock door.

The closed airlock door.

He had almost made it. He had run so hard through the length of the terminal that sweat trickled down his ribs beneath his uniform jacket. He didn't remember it, but at some point he must have puked in his mouth just a little because the taste of bile was thick on his tongue still and his throat burned from more than just gasping for air.

He had thought he was in pretty good shape up until a minute ago.

Now he had no idea what he was going to do. For the moment, it was enough to rest his sweaty forehead against the cool metal of the airlock door and get his breathing back under control before the stitch in his side dug in any deeper.

He heard a soft hiss of air, but before he could begin to get curious as to where it was coming from, he was spilling into the airlock.

Which had no room for him. Even so, entirely too many sets of hands were grabbing fistfuls of his uniform and dragging him into the tight space. Somehow, they got him wedged in before the door shut again.

"You cut that one close," a large red-headed guy, also in a cadet's uniform, said. But Fitz was mostly tucked into the big guy's armpit and couldn't get a proper look at his face.

The young woman closest to the door controls, he could see. They had made eye contact briefly before the door closed. In that instant, he had been sure he was imagining things, but now he knew he wasn't.

It *was* Murdina Ritchie. His old childhood friend, here of all places. And also in a cadet uniform, the brown hair that had always reached past her waist now cut short, just starting to curl out from behind her ears.

They had never gotten a chance to say goodbye after that day where everything when so wrong with her father's mission. For the first few years afterwards, he had obsessed about what he would say when he did see her again. How to convey all of his feelings into words that didn't cross the lines his father had drawn. It had felt impossible, but throwing himself at the challenge over and over again had felt like a kind of penance. The only penance he would be allowed to do.

Then more years passed and, although she had never slipped from his memory, he had come to accept their paths were never going to cross again. He had felt his father's hand in that, too.

But now here she was, and he was completely unprepared. What fourteen-year-old him had come up with during all those sleepless nights wasn't going to cut it now.

No, the best plan would be to wait for her to say something first.

Only she wasn't even looking at him now. Was it possible she hadn't recognized him?

"Come through," a commanding older man's voice said, and a petite blonde cadet he hadn't even noticed until that moment squirmed out from behind him to join the man in the corridor on the far side of the airlock.

"Colonel..." Fitz started to say. He could see the man's rank, but not his name.

"Cadet," the colonel said, catching the red-headed cadet by the arm to pull him out of the airlock. Then he leaned in to loom over Fitz. Still in the corridor, he was a big step up from the airlock floor, a necessity if he wanted to loom over Fitz.

"Cadet Shackleton Fitz IV, sir," Fitz said. The colonel's eyes narrowed, and Fitz guessed he didn't like to be interrupted.

"I know who you are," the colonel said darkly. His tone made it clear he was talking about more than Fitz's name.

He went on from there, at great length and with a wide and colorful vocabulary, about punctuality and related topics. Fitz's mind instantly tuned the words out. He had been bawled out enough at his other schools to know it was just best to wait until a response was wanted. He tried his best to look contrite, but that had never been part of his skill set.

Out of the corner of his eye, he saw Ritchie, all but trembling as she made herself as small as possible in the corner of the airlock. The colonel didn't seem to notice she was still in there, but she was reacting as if she were the one getting yelled at.

A fleck of spittle on his cheek drew his attention back to the colonel, still venting his spleen. Fitz kept his gaze mostly unfocused, but couldn't help but notice the silvery lines of old scars tracing over the olive skin of the colonel's face. What action had he seen? Was it why he was now on his way to the Oymyakon Foreign Service Academy?

This particular academy was the lowest of the low, the furthest from anything like civilization, with no one of note on the faculty and no access to anything beyond the barest rudimentary training. Its name carried no prestige whatsoever.

Fitz had nearly missed the train on account of his father insisting on speaking to him by private holo just to let him know one last time what a black mark this academy's name would be on Fitz's record. That had been followed up by dark threats of the consequences of getting the blacker mark of being flunked out of the last possible academy that would take him, his future as an officer dead before it could even begin.

Most of that Fitz had tuned out, but he knew the broad strokes, having heard it many times before. If the Oymyakon Foreign Service Academy was a step down for him, a screwup kid, what did that say about the faculty that were assigned there?

He glanced at Ritchie again. Why was *she* going there?

And why did the airlock smell so strongly of caramel? It was making him hungry.

The colonel had not yet started to flag in his dressing down when he was interrupted by a young man in a steward's uniform touching his arm with extreme caution, as if he were afraid he was about to lose a hand.

"Sir?" the steward said.

The colonel closed his eyes, then turned calmly to the steward. "Yes?"

"We've undocked, sir," the steward said.

"Yes, I did notice that," the colonel said. Now that the officer's attention was no longer fixed on him, Fitz was able to direct his attention to the name tag. Colonel... Hansen, then. Not a familiar name, but that didn't mean much. It was a big universe.

"Sir, I took the liberty of summoning the steward who is assigned to your car, Feliks Novikov." He took a slight step back and an even younger man bounced up on tiptoe to be seen over the first steward's shoulder. Feliks had thick hair, a sun-bleached blond that was darker at the roots but currently fiercely combed back into a tidy style that in no way suited him.

"There are four of you?" Feliks asked, looking from Fitz and the colonel to the redhead and blond standing in the corridor with him.

"No, five," the colonel said with a frown, looking around until he spotted Ritchie in the corner. She flushed and raised a hand as if marking herself present at roll call.

"Excellent," Feliks said. "If you'll follow me?"

"Buddy up," the colonel said as he stepped out of the airlock to fall into step beside Feliks. Ritchie scrambled up after him, the blonde girl waiting for her to reach her side before following the colonel and the steward.

The red-headed cadet extended a hand and Fitz took it, more to show his appreciation for the gesture than from any actual need. The steward looked back at them to make sure they were all following, then turned back to say something to the colonel beside him.

Fitz saw a wink of light, something small flashing from the back of

Feliks' ear. It was just a speck of a thing, mostly hidden behind the flesh of his ear and covered by a carefully arranged wave of hair, but Fitz recognized it all the same. He had seen similar jewels the last time he had been at the beach on Rangeela 8. The colors were supposed to mean something about what he was up for party-wise or what he was looking for in a mate, Fitz didn't really remember. It wasn't an affectation taken up by any in his circle.

Still, it told him a bit about Feliks. That might come in handy over the next few days on the train, his last days of semi-freedom.

The corridor stretched on past door after door, most closed but a few open to a view of various occupants settling into their cabins or just sitting in their seats watching the swarm of shuttles and larger vessels as they drifted towards or away from the depot. Nothing Fitz hadn't seen before.

When they reached the end of the car, Feliks opened the door to the next car, then looked back again to make sure they all were still following him.

They were all going to be in a group the entire trip, and once they got to the academy, who knew what would happen then? If he was going to find a moment to talk to Ritchie even semi-privately, it was going to have to be now.

So Fitz let the red-head step through first into what appeared to be another car of sleeper cabins with another long corridor passing between doors. Then he stretched out a hand to catch Ritchie's wrist and tug her back behind the big red-headed fellow. She snatched her hand away and glared at him, but let the redhead stay in front of her.

"Hey," Fitz said. As opening lines went, not his best, but at least when she was looking at him, it was with recognition.

"Hey, yourself," Ritchie said, rubbing her wrist as if he might have left a mark.

He needed to lighten the mood. That *was* part of his skill set. He grinned as he looked over at her out of the corners of his eyes. "You were thinking about it, for a moment there. Weren't you?" Fitz asked.

"Thinking about what? When?" she asked.

"You saw me running to the train," he said.

"Yes, and I opened the airlock door back up to let you in," she said.

"You did," he admitted, then jostled her gently with his elbow. "But for a minute there—"

"Don't be ridiculous," she scoffed. "Why would I do such a thing? Pointless mischief was always more your thing."

"That's true," he said. Then added, "you look different."

"I should hope so. It's been four years," she said, but he could see a flush of pink coloring her cheeks.

"I like your hair," he said.

"Oh," she said, touching the ends of it. "It's new. For the academy." Then she looked over at him assessingly. "You're the same."

"I got a bit taller," he said.

The others had reached the end of the car and Feliks was waiting for them to catch up before moving on to the next one. Ritchie hurried her steps and Fitz did the same, mostly to keep up with her. He had so much more to say to her, if he could find the words.

But the next car was an observation car, the walls and ceiling transparent to provide an unfettered view of space all around them. Fitz glanced up and back to follow the curvature of the train past the bridge car to the massive ring of the jump drive, waiting for them to navigate into its center and dock within it. He had made similar journeys dozens of times in the last year alone, but judging from the way Ritchie's mouth hung open in awe, she had not.

"Didn't you leave Buennagel by train?" he asked.

Not how he had wanted to bring up how she had left without the two of them ever saying goodbye, but it was too late to take it back.

Ritchie closed her mouth and looked away from the spacescape around them. At first he thought she was going to ignore the question, or maybe even walk away from him without answering it. But then she shot him the briefest of glances and, whatever she saw in his face, decided to give some sort of answer.

"I didn't leave my cabin much that trip," she said. She wouldn't look at him, but he could feel the dread that he would press her for more details coming off of her in waves.

He said no more. He could well imagine how upset she and her mother had been, especially those first chaotic days when no one knew for sure what had happened or what any of it was going to mean.

When they passed out of the observation car and into the reading car with its tables, chairs, and arrays of readers left out for quiet use, he saw her look around with interest again, taking in all the details. It went beyond being ordinary to him to a level of actual boredom, but she was clearly fascinated by all of it.

For that matter, so was the red-headed cadet. Only the blonde cadet looked as unimpressed as Fitz felt.

The colonel and the steward hustled them through the saloon car as if the mere smell of alcohol on the air around them would have some corrupting influence. Not even Fitz was foolhardy enough to try to sneak off to here during the journey, and the pointed glance Colonel Hansen threw his way irked him.

But a lot of passengers wanted a little something before they reached jumpspace, and the saloon was crowded. People gathered around too-small tables, failing to accommodate for everyone else's jutting elbows, all trying to talk louder than any of the others to be heard over the din. Nope, definitely not his scene either.

The next car was the tearoom. There was no enforced rule of quiet here, like in the reading car, but the passengers who preferred it to the saloon seemed disinclined to shout at each other. Tea wasn't really his thing, but the pyramidal stacks of little cakes were tempting.

Finally, they reached what Fitz knew was the central car of the train, because on every train he'd ever been on, the formal dining room was always the central car. This one didn't disappoint, every table draped in champagne-colored fabric, the china and cutlery the staff were still arranging as the cadets passed through gleaming richly in the warm light from the hovering chandeliers above. The high-vaulted ceiling beyond was cut with windows that offered fleeting glimpses of the space around them. What looked like wandering stars were just the lights from shuttles too far off for their outlines to be seen.

Then that view was blotted out as something overtook them from behind, the massive ring of the jump drive all that could be seen as the train drifted into its very center. They had jumped on board the train near the front end, and Fitz was beginning to suspect they were going to walk the entire length of it before they got to their cabin.

The next car was an informal diner, the only windows small and set low over the surface of the tables of the booths that ran down both sides of the car. Everything was shining red or dazzling chrome, clean and bright, and the aroma of fried food lingered in the air, memories of meals past. His stomach, already rumbling since the tea cakes, gave a louder growl.

He felt the light touch of fingertips on his arm and looked up, then jumped as he realized it was no longer Ritchie walking beside him but the blonde cadet. Even with her hair piled up in a tall topknot, she didn't quite reach his shoulder, and he resisted the urge to bend over towards her to bring his ear down to her level.

"I've been waiting for you to say hello, but I'm starting to think you're not going to," she said with a twinkle in her dark blue eyes.

That shade of blue had to be fake. No way real eyes came in that deep of an azure.

"Sorry?" he said, trying for casual and not the flustered confusion he was actually feeling.

"You haven't said hello," she said again.

"Hello," he said, knowing that wasn't remotely what she was looking for, but still. She must be mistaking him for someone else.

"Shackleton Fitz IV," she said in a chiding tone. So much for that theory. "Don't you remember me?"

"Of course I remember you," he said. They left the diner car behind and found themselves in another reading room, this one quite empty. There would be another observation car before they got to the sleeper car, and who knew how many of those there would be?

"No, you don't," she said, but she didn't sound offended. "We've met at dozens of parties."

"I do go to a lot of parties," Fitz said. The redheaded cadet turned to look back at the two of them, something inscrutable but not exactly friendly in his eyes.

"You were at Marilin Stover's cabana on Rangeela 8 last equinox day," the blonde girl went on.

"Lots of people were at Marilin's last equinox."

"Okay, smart guy," she said, the twinkle still in her eye as she shot a look up at him. "Guy Travert took a bunch of us out for a spin on his space yacht when his trust fund money came in. You were there, and so was I."

"Again," Fitz said, holding up his hands in mock surrender, "lots of people."

"I was even at a *Fitz* party," she said. "Last winter on Buennagel. For an entire week while your parents were on vacation."

"I remember that party," Fitz groaned. "I got in so much trouble for that party. Totally worth it, though." He looked down at her again, trying to imagine her face with different hair, or maybe different eyes. Some kids liked to change their appearance up at a whim. But there was absolutely nothing familiar about her. "I'm sorry, I really don't remember you."

She just shrugged, unbothered. "It's Antoinette Moreau."

"Pleased to meet you," he said with a nod of his head. "This time I'm committing that to memory, I swear."

"I would hope so," she said. "There are only four of us, and her you clearly already know."

"Ritchie?" he said. "Yeah, I know Ritchie."

"But I'm guessing not Weld," she said. The redhead looked back at them again.

"You're Weld?" Fitz said to him.

"Cadmar Weld," the hulking fellow said. Fitz wasn't used to guys his age making him feel small. Weld only had a few centimeters of height on him, but he was easily twice as wide. "I haven't been to any of your parties."

"No, I don't suppose so," Fitz said. But that was the wrong thing to say when one wanted to make new friends. "Not yet, anyway," he hastily amended.

Weld turned to face front again without a word, but Fitz was pretty sure his gesture had just been rejected.

"Here we are," Feliks said as he opened the door to another sleeper car.

"Just the one car on this end?" the colonel asked with a frown. They had passed through five beside the VIP car on the other end of the train.

"This one plus another VIP car behind it," Feliks said as he led the way down the corridor. "The train breaks up after the jump, and most of the passengers won't be going on to Oymyakon. Just these last two cars."

"When does the train split apart?" Ritchie asked.

"In the night," Feliks said. "There's really not much to see, even from the observation cars, but if you want me to wake you, I can."

"No, that's okay," Ritchie said, flushing again.

"As you wish," Feliks said, then stopped to open one of the doors. "Colonel Hansen, this is your cabin here."

"And the cadets?" he asked, glaring at the four of them as if they had already broken a rule.

"Just down there," Feliks said, pointing at a door further down and on the other side of the train.

"Very well," the colonel said. "Settle in, cadets, but stay in your cabin. I'll fetch you when it's time for dinner and we'll pass back down the train to the dining car together."

"Yes, sir," they all said together.

The colonel went into his cabin and shut the door. Feliks gave the four of them a conspiratorial wink and led the way to the door he had pointed out, but before he reached it, he was stopped by a young woman with dark brown hair in a crown braid, also dressed as a steward.

"Feliks!" she cried out as if undyingly happy to see him.

"Tassa," he said, and the tops of his ears turned just a bit red.

"I need to borrow your cleaning robot," she said. "Please don't ask why."

"Of course," he said, cocking a thumb back over his shoulder, presumably indicating the location of the robot and not the four cadets gathered behind him. "But seriously. Why?"

"I'm not kidding!" she said with a laugh. "You really don't want to know." Then, just as she was brushing past him, Fitz could hear her whisper into his ear, "I'll tell you later."

Feliks gave himself a little shake, then smiled at the four of them before opening the door to their cabin.

"That was Tassa Sokolov," he said, pitching his voice low. "She's the steward for the VIP car. With the passengers we get, especially on the Oymyakon run, there's not enough money in the world to convince me to do that job."

"Demanding, are they?" Fitz asked.

Feliks just rolled his eyes. Then he herded them into the cabin with a pair of bunk beds on each side, the top two folded up against the walls and the bottom two set in seat configuration. A table that folded against the wall was currently opened out into the room just under the window.

"This button summons me if you need anything," Feliks said, touching a spot near the door.

"No in-cabin replicator?" Moreau asked with a frown.

"Not on this train line," Feliks said. "But I can get anything you need for you."

"Can we go back to the observation car?" Ritchie asked.

"Technically yes," Feliks said. "But we're going to jump in half a minute, and there won't be anything worth seeing after that. But tomorrow after we reach Oymyakon, I really recommend the final observation car. You have to take the tunnel under the last VIP car to get there, but then you're at the back of the train and the view is really spectacular."

"We'll keep that in mind," Moreau said, then gave him a pointed look until he took the hint and left with a nod.

The minute the door hissed shut, it was like they all could finally relax. Weld dropped into the seat closest to the door and rubbed at his eyes as if exhausted after some long mental effort. Ritchie sat beside him but as close to the window as she could get, pressing her face to the glass in an attempt to see even more of the blackness of space within the confines of a jump drive ring.

Moreau settled into the seat across from Ritchie and watched her looking out the window with an air of deep amusement.

Apparently, Ritchie felt those eyes on her because she looked up. "Sorry, but this is all so exciting. Isn't it?"

Moreau gave a little scoffing laugh. "Is it?" she countered. "Because I imagine we're about to live through the longest, dullest two days in my life. Of course, I don't know about yours."

Ritchie didn't seem to know how to respond to that, so Fitz jumped in the conversational gap. "Dull is good," he said, slumping into his own seat as if settling into a nap which he didn't remotely need. "With space travel, dull is always good."

3

AS EXCITED as she was to get a glimpse of anything at all, Ritchie finally had to admit that there was really nothing to see outside the window. She knew the train was docking with the jump drive ring, and occasionally she could feel something vibrating the seat under her and the wall and the window she was pressed against. She imagined it was some sort of docking mechanism extending out from the train locking on to something similar extending in from the ring.

Of course, she had always been more interested in people and culture than ships and structures, so she knew what she was picturing was vague and probably incorrect. She wished she could see it, but she couldn't make out a single detail outside of a few winking lights that were shuttles moving through space far beyond the front end of the train.

Then, after one last barely sensed clang, an orange light winked on over the doorway.

"What does that mean?" Ritchie asked.

"We're about to jump," Fitz said, without opening his eyes. He untucked one arm to reach for the control panel by the door. "I can turn the voice notifications on if you like?"

"She can do that with her own implant if she's that curious,"

Moreau said, getting up from her seat to reach up for the knob on the bottom of the window blind.

"Don't close it," Ritchie said.

"I'm sorry, I know this is all exciting and new for you, but some of us get sick looking out at jump space," Moreau said. She raised herself up on the very tips of her toes but still couldn't reach the knob.

"I'll get it," Weld said, getting up from his seat to reach past her.

"Give it a minute," Fitz said, still pretending to be napping. "Moreau can cover her eyes long enough for Ritchie to have a look see."

Ritchie looked up at Weld, who appeared torn.

"Have you ever seen jump space?" she asked him.

"On the way here," he said. "I didn't like it."

"Normal people don't," Moreau said.

"I just want a quick look," Ritchie said. "The shuttle I flew to the depot on had no windows in the passenger area at all."

"Fine," Moreau huffed, and threw herself back down on her seat. Weld stood ready to pull down the blind, his eyes on Ritchie.

There was a lurch, as if the train had started to move forward but braked hard at the last moment. Not something that objects in space generally do, but Ritchie had no idea what else she was feeling happening. Moreau groaned from behind the hands pressed to her face, and Ritchie realized the blackness beyond the window was no longer the shadow cast by the massive jump drive ring. In fact, she couldn't see the ring at all. No, this darkness was something else, a more total blackness that seemed to press against the window like inky water at the bottom of a sea. No light, but massive pressure.

So that was jump space. The concept was mind-bending, but the actual visual was underwhelming.

"It doesn't look like anything," she said, disappointed.

"That's because it isn't anything," Moreau said. "It's nothing. It's something beyond nothingness. I hate it."

Her hands were still pressed to her face. Ritchie looked out the window again. She felt a vague uneasiness when she imagined the entire train was at the bottom of an ocean with water all around ready to squash them all like bugs the moment the hull ruptured and failed.

But when she pushed that image from her mind, it was just like any other darkness. Why did it bother Moreau so much?

"You sound like you travel a lot for someone who reacts to jump space this badly," Weld said.

"I usually medicate," Moreau said into her hands. "Is it closed yet?"

Ritchie gave Weld a little nod, and he pulled the blind down, locking it in place.

"It's closed," he said as he sat back down.

Moreau waited a moment, as if to be sure they weren't pulling a prank on her before lowering her hands.

"Weld has a point," Fitz said, and Ritchie saw he had given up pretending to nap.

"What's that?" Moreau asked.

"You're pursuing a career that's going to call for lots of travel," he said. "Odd for someone with such an adverse reaction."

"I haven't let it stop me yet," Moreau said.

"Still, are you hoping for a permanent posting in the capital stations or something?" Fitz asked.

Moreau gave him a wry smile. "Actually, I don't have any particular career path in mind. I only signed up to annoy my mother. Mission accomplished."

"You enrolled in a foreign service academy just to annoy your mother?" Ritchie asked, not bothering to hide just how appalled she found that concept.

"I know, I know. I'm meant to focus on the 'service', right?" Moreau said.

"No. I mean... I guess?" Ritchie said. She realized she was stammering and shut her mouth.

"So you're a new cadet, not a transfer," Fitz said. Moreau nodded.

"Me too," Weld said, raising a finger.

"And me," Ritchie said. "I'd pretty much given up hope of getting in anywhere. Some cadets start at the beginning of sophomore year, but I've never heard of anyone starting halfway through the first semester of sophomore year."

"That's why I assumed we were all transfers," Fitz said. "Well, I guess congratulations to all of you for getting in at the last possible opportunity."

"Congratulate us when we don't wash out," Weld said with a worried frown.

"I'm not washing out," Moreau said.

Ritchie wished she had half of Moreau's confidence.

She *had* had that kind of confidence, once. Before her initial batch of applications to start as a freshman at any academy at all had all been rejected. She hadn't given up. She had been following an extreme regimen of physical training for years, and no one she knew studied harder than she did.

But those rejections haunted her. Her best hadn't been good enough before. What if it wasn't good enough now?

"Stick close to me, Weld. I'll see you don't fall behind," Fitz said.

"Oh yeah? How are you going to do that?" Weld asked.

"I've been to more than twelve foreign service academies in the last four years," Fitz said.

"Four years?" Weld said with a frown. "Either you're older than you look—"

"Or he was in the understudy program," Moreau interrupted.

Weld's eyebrows went up. "That's a prestigious program. They only take really exceptional applicants." Then his mouth opened and closed a few times as he started but cancelled several follow-up lines of thought. Ritchie smiled. Clearly, he didn't know how to point out that Fitz didn't strike any of them as an exceptional applicant.

"They're usually kids with multicultural backgrounds," Ritchie filled in. "Or the exceptionally bright."

"Or those with a really important parent or two," Moreau said.

Fitz shrugged nonchalantly. Weld looked from Moreau to Fitz and back again twice. Then he turned back to Fitz, his brow furrowing in confusion.

"If you're that talented, why twelve academies?"

Moreau put a hand over her mouth to stifle a laugh, but Fitz was as unbothered as ever.

"I think you're missing the subtext," Fitz said, leaning forward to speak more directly to Weld, although in the tiny confines of the cabin,

Ritchie and Moreau could hear him perfectly well. "My Very Important Paterfamilias pulled oh so many strings to get me into that prestigious program, displacing some other qualified candidate who surely would have used the opportunity to mold themselves into a future servant of the Union of Free Worlds who could really accomplish something. But I both didn't deserve the honor and didn't want it."

"But you couldn't turn it down," Moreau said, as if she knew the feeling well. "Or even flunk out of it, apparently."

"No, that was never an option," Fitz said. "The best I could do was to wear out a place. But my father could always find another place willing to take me."

"And this helps me how?" Weld asked. "I don't need pointers on how to fail."

"I know *how* to succeed," Fitz said. "Better than anyone, since I have gotten so good at avoiding it. And I'd be the best possible coach, since I have no desire to compete with you."

"I don't know," Weld said.

"Well, think about it," Fitz said with another careless shrug. "But in the end, I think you'll come around. I'm a likable guy."

"He is," Moreau agreed.

Ritchie found herself pressed against the blinded window again, this time out of an unconscious desire to no longer be in the same cabin as this conversation. But as usual, she couldn't keep her thoughts quietly to herself. "Don't you ever think about that other kid?" she asked.

"What kid?" Fitz asked.

"The one trying to get into the understudy program whose place you took," Ritchie said. "The one who deserved it. The one who probably would have tried."

"It's not like anyone can tell me their name," Fitz said. "It's hard to feel bad about the concept of a kid. Besides, I had no more choice in any of this than they did."

"You could have chosen to make the best of the opportunity and *try*," Ritchie said.

Before Fitz could respond, the door to the cabin slid open, the colonel standing in the corridor.

"Time for dinner," he said, and they all got to their feet.

All thoughts of Fitz squandering his opportunities left her head as Ritchie followed the others back through the train to that magnificent formal dining room. She couldn't believe she was actually going to sit there at one of those gorgeously golden tables under the floating chandeliers and eat a multicourse dinner with all of those elaborate pieces of cutlery. She had expected nothing more than ration packs in the cabin, just the four of them.

The windows in the dining car, as in the observation car they passed through, were opaqued to shut out the sight of jump space. Instead, holograms of color patterns danced over their surfaces, reminding her of the one of the nebula over the terminal back at the depot.

The five of them were shown to one of the tables near the center of the car. The chairs had tall backs with wings designed to close off the space around the round table, giving them a small measure of privacy, or at least the illusion of it. But it also had the effect of making Ritchie feel small and child-like.

Or maybe she felt like a child because the sound of golden forks and knives on porcelain plates and the clink of crystal glasses against each other brought back the memory of state dinners she had attended when her father had still been an up-and-coming diplomat for the Union of Free Worlds. There had only been a few of them when she was old enough to attend before he had been taken away, but she remembered them each fondly. She had loved the pomp, the structured formality of which fork to use and what order the food was eaten in. She had studied every conversation happening around her for all that was said and unsaid, to discuss her impressions with her father later.

She had so looked forward to a life of that. It had all gone away so quickly.

She was sitting with Weld on her left and Fitz on her right, but there was a gap between Weld's chair and the colonel's, so when Weld started mumbling angrily under his breath, she was the only one to hear.

"What is it?" she leaned closer to him to ask. "It's just the five of us;

I'm sure the colonel won't mind if you need a little help on the table etiquette."

"I know how to eat," Weld growled at her. Then he closed his eyes and took a deep breath. "Sorry. It's not you. It's *her*."

"Her?" Ritchie whispered back, glancing over at Moreau, who was fussing with her napkin under the table.

"Not her," Weld said, then pointed with his chin. "Her."

Ritchie looked through the gap between Moreau's chair and Fitz's. The party at the next table was just getting settled in, although there seemed to be something amiss, as the server pulled out a chair the woman before him refused to sit in.

If it was possible for a woman to look like an old, massive warship, this woman did it. Ritchie wasn't sure if it was the way her broad shoulders and heavy bosom made her look like she was prepared to batter down any obstruction, or the way her steel gray hair was aggressively styled into an updo that somehow looked sharp, but the effect was impossible to dismiss.

She didn't blame the hapless server from quailing as she berated him.

"Who is she?" Ritchie whispered.

"That," Weld said sourly, "is the Lady Marie-Claire Fabron. From the planet of Loindetu."

"Loindetu," Ritchie repeated, casting back through her memory. She had studied every planet in the Free Worlds at some point, but there were so many it took her a moment to call up any information on it. "Fourth quadrant?"

"Yes," Weld said.

"They were put on probation by the Union," Ritchie said, as what she had read started coming back to her. "They violated the nonexpansion rules, trying to conquer neighboring worlds to colonize them. But that ended, right?"

"The probation ended," Weld said.

Another man stepped up to the Lady Fabron. He was a short, slender man with dark black skin and a shaved scalp. At first glance, Ritchie thought from how smoothly he moved that he was quite young, but as he looked up at the lady, she saw his face was quite wrinkled. He spoke to the lady and then to the server and finally whatever the problem had been was cleared up and she took her seat. The dark-skinned man took a seat across from her, his back to Ritchie and Weld, so that he was effectively out of their view.

Then the server pulled out another chair and something that had been hidden from view behind the table hopped up to sit at the Lady Fabron's elbow.

"What is that?" Weld asked, repulsed. "Some kind of animal?"

The thing did look like an animal, covered as it was with honey-colored fur. But it also looked like a particularly pudgy human toddler, one with over-sized eyes that were also the color of honey. It looked up at the lady adoringly as the server quickly cleared everything but the plate and spoon from its place setting.

"A pet, I guess?" Ritchie asked.

"You two are driving me mad," Fitz said. "What is so fascinating directly behind me?"

"The Lady Fabron, widow of Admiral Fabron," Weld said in a low growl.

"Ah," Fitz said with a knowing nod. "And you're also from the fourth quadrant, I take it?"

"Fallon 5," Weld said.

Fitz let out a low whistle. "Did you lose anyone that day?"

"Just my home," Weld said. "No one could ever directly link the illnesses that killed my grandparents to the chemical warfare."

"I'm so sorry," Ritchie said.

"It wasn't you," Weld said.

"Well, it wasn't her either," Fitz said diplomatically. "It was her husband, and almost certainly under orders."

Weld narrowed his eyes. "It was a war crime. And it was her husband, and all five of her sons, and however many more extended members of her family. And maybe they were all following orders. But her face was on all the propaganda that rained down on us. She was the one always telling us how happy we'd be under the loving guidance of Loindetu military rule."

"Cadet Weld," the colonel said, his voice carefully pitched to reach the ears of everyone at the table, but no further. "Drop it." Weld's lips compressed into a thin, angry line. "I don't doubt that your griev-ances are just, but this isn't the place to air them. Understood, cadet?"

"Yes, sir," Weld said.

The server directed an array of drones to place their first course on their plates. Ritchie could sense the turmoil still roiling through Weld beside her, but he made a good outward show of focusing on his food.

The drones had just come back to deliver the second course when a murmur of voices had Ritchie looking up again through the gap between Moreau's and Fitz's chairs.

A man was standing at the Lady Fabron's elbow, a cap in his hands as he gave her a little bow. He was dressed in civilian clothes, but Ritchie could see the bearing of a career military officer in the way the man stood and how he moved. But the clothes were not quite ordinary civilian things either. The dark colors and convenient pockets and tactical cut were not quite military, and after a moment Ritchie decided he was returning from a hunting expedition, or heading off to one. Oymyakon had no native species worth hunting, but perhaps he was heading in a different direction when the train broke apart in the morning after coming out of jump space.

"Do you know who that is?" Ritchie whispered to Weld. Weld looked the man over, but shook his head.

"Apparently she doesn't either," he added, as the Lady Fabron dismissed the man with an imperious wave of her hand.

Then she turned her attention back to the little creature in the chair next to her, cutting off a sliver of meat from the cutlet on her plate and sliding it from her fork to the thing's spoon.

Something about the way the thing seized on the spoon and studiously navigated it into its mouth triggered a memory. Had she seen something like this before? She knew of no one who had such a pet, but perhaps she had seen it in a menagerie in the capital?

Then a little jingly tune ran through her mind and she had it.

"Oh," she said out loud, putting a hand to her mouth.

"What?" Fitz asked, clearly desperate to turn around and look.

"It's a Felzkinder," Ritchie said. "I remember the advertisements from when I was a kid. When I was five, I really, really wanted one. But my dad would never have allowed it. He said it wasn't the sort of thing someone should own."

"It isn't, now," Fitz said with a frown. "They were declared a sentient species. The Union of Free Worlds recognizes them as autonomous beings. I thought they even had an old space station they were declaring their home world."

"Then how is that one still a pet?" Weld asked.

"Loophole," Moreau said. "The older ones display less sentience than the newer models. There is a legal path to keep the older ones if they were pets before the ruling, although I imagine the bureaucracy involved is staggering."

Ritchie took another bite of her roasted meat, but looked up at the little creature again as she chewed. Now that she was looking more closely, she could see many silver hairs in that honey-colored pelt, and even a pattern of wrinkles around its eyes.

But those eyes, when it turned them up at the lady, were a potent combination of a human toddler at its most charming and the sweetest of puppies.

The lady cut off another sliver of meat and slid it onto the bowl of the spoon, and the little Felzkinder clapped its chunky little hands in delight. Ritchie wasn't sure what tests were done to prove a being's sentience, but this one was clearly smart enough to use what it had to get what it wanted. It had almost weaponized its cuteness.

But did it really want to be a pet?

4

FITZ WOKE briefly in the early hours of the morning and knew it was because the train had just come out of jump space. There was no sound, no change in momentum or anything like that to indicate the shift to normal space. It was more like a pressure on his eardrums that he hadn't even been noticing was suddenly gone.

He turned over on his side and slipped back into sleep.

It couldn't have been more than an hour later when he felt the train rattling around him and heard the clang of parts so far off in the distance he was probably just imagining it. The train was breaking up, different parts heading off towards different planets in this quadrant.

Across the cabin in the other top bunk, Ritchie hoisted up on one elbow, her head tipped as she listened. Then she threw back the covers, dropping to the floor without waking Weld or the gently snoring Moreau. She softly detached the blind from the locking mechanism and slid it back up until the window was uncovered. There was nowhere for her to sit with the bottom bunks also in sleep mode, but once she folded the little table against the wall, she could stand as close to the window as she liked.

A starscape was a starscape anywhere in the universe, lovely enough but not terribly interesting. After several moments with her forehead pressed to the cold glass, Ritchie came to the same conclusion and climbed back up into her bunk to go back to sleep.

She had never left Buennagel until the day she left it for good, he reminded himself. Her father had travelled often, consulting at this or that embassy, but he had never taken his family with him. Being a kid at the time, Fitz had never thought much of it. But it seemed odd to him now. Most people moved about for work or pleasure, visiting family or just enjoying exotic locations.

Where had Ritchie gone after her father had been taken? Where had she been this entire time? And why did the entire universe still seem like a new experience to her?

When he woke for the third time, it was to find the cabin bathed in a bluish light. He sat up and saw Ritchie once more awake with her face pressed to the window. She was in full uniform now, her bunk tucked up against the wall.

Fitz climbed down out of his own bunk, as silently as he could so as to not wake Moreau and Weld. Ritchie glanced back at him but quickly went back to looking out the window.

He leaned in close behind her to look out over her shoulder. He could still see the curvature of the planet they were closing in on, but only on the very edges of the field of view. The thinnest wisps of atmosphere were closing around them, and the train was buffeted every so often.

"Not much to see," Fitz said, whispering close to her ear.

"It's my second planet," Ritchie told him. "After Buennagel."

"This one? That's a shame," he said.

"Why's that?" she asked.

"Are you kidding me? You must have done *some* research," he said.

"I know it's habitable," she said. "But I guess not pleasant. Have you been here before?"

"No," he said. "But you realize we'll be circling around a perpetual storm for days. We're going to be dropping in through the calmest patch the navigator can spot, no matter where on the planet that might be, and then chugging along under the storm by whatever route is passable."

"I did know that," Ritchie said. "It's why we had to take a train. No spaceports on Oymyakon."

"And no scheduled arrival times once we get there," Fitz said.

"Well, it doesn't vary so much as all that," Ritchie said. "From what I've read, they don't have to deviate more than an hour or two to get around most storms."

"But you're not thinking ahead," Fitz said. "Once we get off this train, we'll be on the ground. In one place. And just look at those dark gray skies. It will be nothing but that for years."

"I might not be the best judge of how terrible that's going to be," Ritchie said. "I haven't seen a real sky in years. Even a stormy sky sounds perfectly lovely to me."

"I guess I'm spoiled," Fitz said.

"You guess?" Ritchie said, and the teasing sparkle in her eye made her almost look like she was the twelve-year-old girl he had known again.

There was a soft knock on the door, which promptly opened before either of them could even turn around. It was Feliks with a tray of covered dishes in his hands.

"Good morning!" Feliks said. "Can you drop that table down for me?"

Fitz and Ritchie found the mechanism to extend the table as Weld and then finally Moreau sat up, yawning and looking around.

"Breakfast?" Weld asked.

"Just a light one," Feliks said, setting the covered dishes on the table one by one, then tucking the tray under his arm.

"The dining room isn't open?" Moreau asked.

"Not just now. The Oymyakon atmosphere can be a bit choppy," Feliks said, in a tone of voice that Fitz was sure meant that the "a bit" was a lie.

"Too bumpy for proper dishes?" Moreau said.

"Yes, but also some travelers find it not the best for digestion," he said. "So it's just toast and a fruit sauce for now. You can decide at lunchtime how hungry you are. And of course dinner will be a full service."

"Thanks, Feliks," Ritchie said, and Feliks gave her a little bow before slipping back out of the room.

"Huh," Weld said, leaning past Ritchie to see out the window. "This is Oymyakon? It's just sort of a big gray blob."

"I would ask if your planet is nicer, but I guess after last night, we all know how insensitive that would be," Fitz said. Weld gave him a dark look but then lightened up without Fitz having to explain he had been joking.

"Yes," Weld said. "It was nicer. Not so much now. I've been living in a space station since I was five, but I still remember what it was like being under a sky."

"Well, it's only for a few years," Moreau said, wrinkling her nose at her first look at the planet, too. "Then we'll be at the Foreign Service Universities on Braga. Both schools are right in the sweet spot where it's never too hot and never too cold. The days are always sunny and gentle rains fall at night."

"Sounds like a sales pitch," Fitz said.

"But it's true," Moreau said. "I was visiting some friends of friends last year to hit all the semester break parties and it was gorgeous."

"Something to look forward to, then," Fitz said.

Moreau took the cover off of her plate and heaved a sigh. "It's completely ridiculous the cabins don't have replicators in them."

"Feliks said he'd bring anything you asked for," Ritchie said.

"That's not the point," Moreau said. "Why should I have to ask a person?"

Ritchie looked down at her own plate with a puzzled frown, then glanced over at Weld, who shrugged.

"What is it?" Fitz asked.

"It's just, for most of us, not having access to a replicator is kind of normal," Ritchie said. "We put in requests, and they're fulfilled or not, depending on what the rest of the neighborhood also needs."

"One replicator for the whole neighborhood?" Moreau asked. "And that's what, ten families?"

Weld started choking on a bit of toast and Fitz got up to pound on his back until he coughed it free.

"More, then?" Moreau asked, not amused by Weld's reaction.

"I guess it depends," Ritchie said diplomatically. "Where I lived on one of the satellites of the capital station, it was a thousand people to a replicator. Or so they said; most people think it's much higher than that."

"Same," Weld said between coughs.

"Really," Moreau said, looking at them each closely as if they might be lying to her.

"I'm guessing your family has its own replicator?" Ritchie asked. "I remember that Fitz's does."

"We have..." She looked up and to the left and twitched her fingers as she counted. "Seventeen in our main house. Our summer vacation house has twelve, and our winter vacation house only has nine."

"Only," Weld said with a humorless laugh.

As they had talked and ate the train around them had been jostling more and more violently. Suddenly, it plummeted as if someone had thrown a switch to turn up the gravity to maximum. The last of their breakfast flew up to smash into the ceiling, dropping back down to the table in the next instant as the fall stopped as quickly as it had begun.

"Well, that was exciting," Fitz said, leaning back to push the button to summon Feliks. "If only we had a replicator, I could just make some towels to clean that up."

The skies outside of the window were getting darker and darker as they plunged deeper into the cloud cover.

"I thought we were supposed to find the largest open patch?" Ritchie said.

"Yeah," Fitz said. "I think that's what this is."

A pair of cleaning drones let themselves into the cabin to clean up the mess from the ceiling, tables, walls, floor, and their uniforms. Fitz had been hoping to have a walk around the train and see how many of the cars remained, but the ride was far too turbulent for that to be safe. Instead, the four of them buckled into their seats and retreated into their respective readers.

The Oymyakon Foreign Service Academy had sent them all the coursework they needed to catch up with the rest of the class, and Fitz had tried to dig into it, but even now he couldn't make his mind stay focused. Learning from text was never his thing. He was certain he'd absorb what everyone around him was discussing once he got there and catch up that way. That had worked every time before.

Only this time, he really did intend not to fail. Not because his father had told him not to, but because of what had happened at that last school. For the first time, he had seen that his failure had let other people down, people who were not his father. He swore he wouldn't do that again.

But he doubted he'd be able to focus on words on a reader screen even if the train around him weren't rocking and bouncing as if the pilot had no control over their trajectory whatsoever.

Feliks came back to check on them for lunch, but as he had expected, they all opted not to try eating. The sky outside the window was nearly as dark as jump space, but that only made the random motion that much more vertiginous.

Then the entire cabin was lit up an electric blue, a sustained strobing flash that was still happening when the thunder startled rattling the entire train around them.

"Oh, nearly there now!" Feliks said, as if the entire journey delighted him.

"How can you tell?" Moreau asked.

"This kind of electrical activity is mostly in the lowest level of the atmosphere," he said. "When you see lightning, that means we're almost under the cloud cover."

"Then what?" Ritchie asked.

"Then they deploy the guidance pods," he said. Ritchie looked to Fitz as if he could explain this to her.

"What's a guidance pod?" he asked instead.

"That's how trains get around on Oymyakon," Feliks said. "We're bouncing around a lot up here, but once we're low enough, the pods will anchor us to the ground."

"How?" Weld asked.

"Some sort of field?" Feliks shrugged. "I don't know; I'm just a steward. It doesn't look like anything, although if you look down from the observation car, you can see the pods under us. They pick out the smoothest path through the storms, going ahead to find an anchor point, then pulling up again after the train has passed over them. You'll know when they start working; the whole ride gets smoother. And then there'll be dinner."

"Smoother before dinner sounds good," Moreau said.

"If you want to watch the pods deploy, the observation car in the back of the train is the best spot. You'll feel when they start working," he said.

There was more lightning and thunder for the next hour or so, but then the sky outside the window began to turn a lighter grey. Ritchie tucked her reader away to turn all of her attention to the window, and Fitz gladly did the same, leaning over the table as he was sitting closer to the door.

"Mountains," Ritchie said when she noticed him also looking out the window.

"Nothing but mountains," Fitz said. "The whole planet. Mountains and oceans, although I don't see any of those from here." She leaned in to press her forehead to the thick glass again. "Do you want to go to the back? Maybe we can see more."

"Yes, let's," Ritchie said.

Fitz expected it would be just the two of them, but when they both got to their feet, so did Moreau and Weld. Well, the more the merrier.

The pods clearly hadn't deployed yet, and they had to hold onto the rail that ran the length of the corridor to keep from being shaken off their feet as they walked.

The gaps between the cars were like the airlocks between docked ships, but when they left their sleeper car, they saw not only the door to the next car behind theirs but also another door set at an angle in the floor to the left.

"That way, right?" Ritchie said. "This is the VIP car, and we're not supposed to go through there."

"Normally I'm the most I of the VIPs," Moreau said.

"But not currently," Fitz said, as Ritchie pulled the door open.

As Feliks had said, this was a tunnel that went under the VIP car. There were no windows and only the dimmest of lights, but it was a short walk to where it curved up again into another gap between cars.

And then they were in the observation car at the very end of the train. All the walls were transparent here: top, bottom and sides. Only the rows of reclining chairs on either side marred the view.

Ritchie ran to the very back of the car, past the last pair of chairs, into a sort of bubble that extended out. "I see the pods!" she cried, pointing.

Fitz looked down between his feet at the jagged foothills rushing by below. He could see them too: a series of disks with flashing lights defining their silhouettes, floating down to land on the ground that was a lot further below them than Fitz had first presumed.

So those foothills were mountains. With no towns or vehicles in view, it was hard to grasp the scale.

So the mountain peaks on the horizon were *how* tall?

The train shuddered like a fish caught in a fisherman's grasp, then smoothed out to something pretty close to how it had felt in spaceflight.

"We're on rails from here, I guess," Fitz said. "So to speak."

"I wonder why we avoid the storms once the pods have deployed," Weld said. "It feels so stable compared to a minute ago."

"I think we can assume some trial and error went into that decision," Fitz said. "Let's just be grateful."

"How far to the academy from here?" Ritchie asked, turning to look back over her shoulder. Her eyes widened, and she straightened up, no longer leaning against the glass bubble with her hands pressed around her face to block out the light. Fitz turned as well to see the colonel emerging from the door to the rest of the train.

"Late tomorrow is my understanding," he said as he walked down the aisle between the chairs, looking around with mild interest. "Ready for dinner? They're serving early since no one on the train had lunch."

"Yes, sir!" they all said together.

He gave a little nod, then waved for them to follow him back through the tunnel.

They passed through their own sleeper car, then an empty observation car and a quiet reading car. Beyond that was one of the diner-type cars, although the booths had been folded into the walls in favor of one long white table with gleaming chrome trim surrounded by tall red low-backed chairs.

"No formal dining tonight, sir?" Moreau asked.

"No, that car left with a different part of the train," he said. "There's just one of the saloon cars ahead of us and then the car with the bridge."

"No other passengers were going to Oymyakon?" Weld asked. He was keeping his tone casual, but to Fitz's ears, he was pushing it too hard. He was keenly interested in the answer to that question.

"Oh, a few," the colonel said. "Weld, come sit with me on this side. You three sit across from us."

As they settled into their chairs, Fitz between Moreau and Ritchie, he saw the colonel take a hold of Weld's elbow and speak close to his ear. Weld's ears turned red, but he nodded curtly. Whatever words had passed between them, the colonel appeared satisfied.

The door they had just come through hissed open and they all turned to see the older gentleman come into the diner car. He was dressed like he had been the night before in clothes that looked formal but were clearly designed for ruthless utility.

Someday, when his uniform days were behind him and he could wear whatever he liked, Fitz wanted to dress like that.

The man looked around the long table, saw the colonel and gave a nod. "Colonel Hansen," he said.

"Captain Berger," the colonel said with an answering nod. "I believe we're all eating together this evening."

"How charming," the captain said, sounding as if he found it anything but. He pulled out a chair to sit beside the colonel, then turned his attention to the menu displayed on the tabletop screen.

There was absolutely no way to grill the colonel about the captain without being overheard. Not that he was likely to answer prying questions from a cadet in any event. But still. Fitz had so many questions.

Starting with how the two of them hadn't seemed to know each other when they were all in the dining car the night before, but clearly did now.

The door hissed open again and Fitz turned in his seat to see the Lady Fabron sweeping into the diner car. He rather expected her to turn up her nose at the lower-class surroundings, or the mixing of ranks all around one table, but she seemed no less at home here than she had been in the formal setting the night before.

"Good evening, Lady Fabron," Captain Berger said, getting to his feet and making a little bow. Fitz looked at the colonel, who gave a little shake of his head. Protocol did not dictate the cadets or the colonel should do the same, apparently.

"Good evening," she said in her rich, plummy voice. She looked around as if searching for some sign as to where she should sit. Then the door behind her opened again and her assistant was there, the Felzkinder in his arms.

"Just here, I should think, madam," her assistant said, hustling along the table to pull out the chair next to Ritchie. The lady sat with all the regal grace of a monarch on her throne. The Felzkinder was settled in next to her, and once more every object within its reach was quickly cleared away, this time by the harried assistant.

Fitz watched Ritchie smile politely at the lady and offer her a good evening. Then he saw her eyes dart across the table to where Weld was sitting.

Weld was glowering darkly at the lady and her pet. The colonel cleared his throat, just a simple gesture that didn't seem directed at anyone in particular, but Weld quickly dropped his eyes and focused on the tabletop in front of him.

Fitz was pretty sure he could guess what the colonel had whispered into Weld's ear before. This wasn't the last time he would be expected to dine with a war criminal. Whether he became a diplomat or followed the military path to a career as a guardian, he would have to find a way to be polite to all manner of people he personally held in contempt.

But if that was what the colonel had whispered to him, Fitz thought that not showing his rancor was asking a lot of Weld. It would be very unlikely he would ever again be expected to politely dine with a woman who had been personally involved in the destruction of his planet and the death of his grandparents.

This was going to be a very awkward dinner for all involved.

5

RITCHIE HAD FELT an initial impulse to recoil when the Lady Fabron had seated herself right next to her. But she had studied diplomacy too long to be undone like that. She had conjured up a friendly smile and words of welcome and ignored the daggers Weld's eyes were shooting at her from across the table.

She had expected the lady to ignore her, much as she had dismissed Captain Berger the night before, but she only turned away from Ritchie long enough to get the Felzkinder beside her settled with a spill-proof cup of some milky beverage.

"So you four are cadets, are you?" she asked. Her tone was even haughtier than Moreau's, and Ritchie wouldn't have thought that was possible a second before.

"Yes, we're on our way to the Foreign Service Academy here on Oymyakon," Ritchie said. "Are you familiar with it?"

"Indeed, I am not," the lady said. "As perhaps you know, I did not grow up here. I've only been here for the last handful of years, and I do not leave my estate much. I find it a very gloomy place."

"Your estate?" Ritchie asked.

"Oymyakon," she said with a sniff.

"There weren't many worlds willing to take us exiles in," Captain

Berger said as he frowned down at the menu. "My lady, if what is on offer here isn't to your taste, perhaps I can tempt you with a little of the rorebeast I'm having the staff prepare for me."

"Rorebeast?" the lady said. "Isn't that the aurochs thing they have on Loindetu 7?"

"The planet has reverted to its old name now, Ravvagge or something ridiculous like that, but yes," the captain said. "I served there in my youth and am just coming back from a hunting expedition. It's a sizable roast, more than enough to share all around, and they've been slow cooking it all day. It's a very flavorful meat."

"If you truly don't mind sharing, I would love to try some of that," the colonel said. "I haven't had real meat in ages."

"Certainly, have all you like," the captain said. "Although it doesn't quite top the thrill of the hunt, the joy of sharing the spoils with others is a close second in my heart. All of you, help yourselves."

Ritchie worked to summon a smile of thank you. She had only ever had vat meat before. The idea of eating something that had been roaming a planet minding its own business was a bit stomach-turning. But, she reminded herself, it was part of the job.

"Yes, that does sound lovely," the lady said. "Is it a very tough meat? I only ask because Chou-Chou has trouble with tough meat. His teeth, you know."

"After roasting all day, it will be very tender indeed, I assure you," the captain said, with another one of his little bows.

"Lovely," the lady said again and dismissed the menu with a swipe of one finger.

"So," the captain said, leaning back in his chair and folding his arms over his flat stomach. His eyes went from the colonel to the Lady Fabron—skimming over the cadets completely—and then on to the lady's assistant, sitting on the far side of the Felzkinder. "I don't believe we've been introduced?" he said.

"That is Baptiste Rose," the lady said, and the slender man gave a little bob of his head. "He has served the Fabron family since he was quite a young fellow."

"Six years old," Mr. Rose said. "I was a war orphan, taken in by the late Lord Fabron and brought up in their household."

"Which world?" the captain asked.

"Garovla," Mr. Rose said.

"Ah, Loindetu 3," the captain nodded. "Of course, we're not supposed to call that anymore."

"I assure you I take no offense," Mr. Rose said.

"Such correctness with terms," the lady said with a sniff. "Surely we all know which world is meant no matter the name."

She glanced over at Ritchie, as if looking for validation. Ritchie started to nod politely but caught herself just in time, glancing across the table at the colonel for guidance.

"Of course, as a representative of the Union of Free Worlds, I'm meant to speak against colonization," the colonel said blandly. "But there is little need for such lectures in the present company."

"Quite so," the lady said. "Your Union made your feelings on the matter quite clear."

"No need to rub in the victory," Fitz said, and Ritchie felt her cheeks flaming, even though the words hadn't been hers.

She'd only been thinking them. The lady and the captain seemed pretty oblivious to just what crimes got them exiled from their home world in the first place.

The arrival of the salad course steered the discourse in a less fraught direction. Ritchie found herself only having to agree with the lady that the greens were very fresh, and the dressing was indeed a touch on the rich side.

Then came the roasted rorebeast, served with generous helpings of crisply roasted root vegetables. Ritchie forced herself to taste a bit of the meat and found, to her consternation, that she very much liked it.

"I took the liberty of ordering a dessert for us all to share," the lady Fabron announced as soon as the plates from the main course were cleared. "It is a delicacy of my world: blood-cherry cake."

"My lady," the captain said. He sounded legitimately moved by the gesture. "This is a treat. How did you find blood-cherries? I haven't had any since the war."

"I have a hothouse at my estate," she said. "I eat them fresh all year round. Good for the organs. I think it's the secret to my long life. I don't travel as often as I used to, but when I do, I always bring jars of preserved blood-cherries with me to see me through."

"Oh," the captain sighed as the waitstaff brought in the tall, black cake on a massive platter and set it between the lady and the captain. "How that smell takes me back. And such plump berries."

"Yes, it took a bit of work for my gardeners to get the hang of just what blood-cherries need to grow, but they have it well in hand now," the lady said. "But where is the knife?"

"Here, my lady," Mr. Rose said, getting up from his chair to carefully hand a long, serrated blade to the lady.

"How dense is this cake?" Fitz asked, eyeing the blade that looked more like a sword than a tool for serving desserts.

"Just as dense as it needs to be, cadet Fitz," the lady said sniffily.

Ritchie was impressed. How had she ever learned any of their names?

"It's the blood-cherries, you see," the captain said, leaning forward as the lady, on her feet now, brought the shining blade down to just touch the layer of bulbous cherries that sat atop the cake. Their thick sauce was oozing down the sides of the cake.

Ritchie could see why they were called blood-cherries. The dessert didn't look good to her at all.

"What's the blood-cherries?" Fitz asked.

"The reason for the knife," the captain said. "Their skin is quite resilient. Without a sharp blade, you'll mash them rather than slice neatly through. And one mustn't mash the cherries. It quite ruins the texture of the thing."

The lady brought the blade down. The cherries underneath it were neatly cleaved in two, and as she cut into the cake itself, Ritchie could see that the sauce hadn't just run down the sides. It had soaked through the entire dense interior.

"No, Chou-Chou," the lady said absentmindedly as the Felzkinder attempted to climb up onto the table to reach one of the cherries. She made brushing motions with her hands towards him, which Ritchie found terrifying as she still had that massive knife in her hand, blade dripping with the ichor from the cake. But Chou-Chou was undeterred, attempting to duck around her to get to the confection.

"Really," Captain Berger said. "I don't think these creatures should be allowed among polite society. Certainly not directly on the table-top." He glared down his nose at the creature, the look of disgust on his features morphing into real revulsion when Chou-Chou managed to capture a handful from the side of the cake.

"Chou-Chou is family," the lady said. "He goes where I go." She was drawing herself up to her full height, thrusting out that chest so like a battering prow of a ship. The knife was still in her hand, still looking like she had stabbed someone already with it. It had seemed to dwell there, forgotten, when she'd gestured at Chou-Chou before. Now the tip was rising up ever so slightly.

And not remotely accidentally, Ritchie was sure.

"My apologies, my lady," the captain said with a little bow. "I quite forgot myself."

"I should say you did," the lady sniffed, but finally set the knife aside to settle into her chair with her own slice of cake.

Mr. Rose had, with great difficulty, gotten most of the cake out of the Felzkinder's tight fist, but the moment he had achieved that victory, Chou-Chou darted around his arm to catch another.

Another look of revulsion crossed Captain Berger's face, but the lady was too focused on Chou-Chou to notice, and it was quickly gone.

"Oh, Chou-Chou. No-no!" she tutted. "You know you can't have that, my little one."

Chou-Chou looked at the squashed fistful of cake in his hand and burst into tears.

"I have him, my lady," Mr. Rose said, picking up the Felzkinder to move him away from the cake.

Chou-Chou immediately began to shriek as if Mr. Rose were killing him.

"What's wrong?" Ritchie asked. Under the honey-colored fur, the round cheeks were turning dark red with fury. The little thing was raining blows down on Mr. Rose with such intensity she had no idea how he was not dropping the squirming creature.

"It's quite all right," the lady said. "It is just my Chou-Chou has a bit of a sweet tooth, but blood-cherries will put him quite off his temper. Isn't that so, my little Chou-Chou?"

Chou-Chou ignored her. If anything, he screamed all the louder. Ritchie wondered just how out of temper blood-cherries would make him if *this* was an improvement.

"Mr. Rose, perhaps you had better take your leave," the lady said, her mouth twisting in annoyance.

"Yes, my lady," he said, managing a little bow despite the raging beast in his arms, and all but ran out of the dining car.

"An interesting creature, that," the colonel said.

"I do apologize," the lady said as she presented the colonel with a slice of her cake. "He is normally a perfect dear, but it is my fault for not remembering how he gets at the sight of blood-cherry cake."

Ritchie found the dessert very much not to her liking. The pop of the cherries under her teeth was off-putting, the fruit itself so acerbic she was instantly thirsty. Worse, drinking the last of her water didn't clear the aftertaste from her tongue.

How the thick sauce was so similar to actual blood was too disturbing to allow herself to think about.

She mostly mashed the cake around the plate until it looked like she'd eaten most of it.

Weld, at the end of the table, had never touched his at all.

"Cadets, you are dismissed," the colonel said, and as the four of them got to their feet, he switched his own empty plate for Weld's untouched one and immediately stuffed a large forkful in his mouth.

Ritchie glanced at the lady Fabron, but she was too engrossed in savoring her own slice of cake to notice what was going on at the end of the table.

The moment the door to the dining car hissed shut behind them, Fitz let out a whoosh of air.

"Well, that happened," he said with a grin.

"What happened to *you*?" Ritchie asked. "I'm the one who had to sit next to her and be polite."

"It didn't look like it was hard for you," Weld said with a sneer.

"It was," Ritchie said. "What would it have gained anybody to have been outright rude to her?"

"Dignity?" Weld said. Moreau snorted, although whatever amused her Ritchie had no idea.

"Come, now, Weld," Fitz said amiably. "We all understand how you feel. But you must realize all of us, but Ritchie and the colonel especially, were in there running interference for you. It wouldn't have been proper for you in that uniform to be outwardly hostile to the lady. In the eyes of the Union, she has been exiled, and that is her just punishment for all she has done. That, plus the loss of her entire family. So long as she lives out her days in exile and doesn't attempt to meddle in the politics of the now free world of Loindetu, she needs suffer no more ill will from us."

"Us meaning the Union," Ritchie said. "Not the four of us as private citizens."

"Which we're not," Fitz said. "Not when we're in uniform."

Weld just glowered, but Ritchie sensed he knew they were right. If he wanted a career in foreign service, that was a distinction he would have to learn to make.

But just at the moment, she guessed he was questioning just how badly he wanted that career.

Much later, Ritchie found herself in her bunk, staring at the ceiling that was just in front of her eyes.

The train was running as smoothly as it had the night before. It was actually more pleasant now without that strange feeling of pressure that came from traveling through jump space. So why couldn't she sleep?

It wasn't like her stomach being in knots could be keeping her awake. Because her stomach being in knots was its usual state.

Still, the long evening with the other cadets in their cabin after dinner had been an awkward hang.

Did everything Moreau say contain an array of little digs, or was it just something in her tone that made it sound that way? Had dining with the lady Fabron prompted her to raise her own bar for superciliousness?

Ritchie would think she was being paranoid, but Fitz kept smirking as if he and Moreau were sharing the joke. So there *had* to be a joke. But Ritchie wasn't worldly enough to work it out. Except for when the joke seemed to center on her own famous name. She could always sense those jokes.

No, that had to be her paranoia talking. She was just too used to dreading that the people around her were about to find out who she was, who her father was, why their last name sounded familiar. She had kept most of her classmates back on the satellite station from ever knowing that bit of her back story.

Now she was traveling with four people who knew, and they weren't her mother or her grandmother. This was new territory for her. It made sense that she was having trouble figuring out how to navigate it.

Ritchie turned onto her side and forced her eyes to shut. She didn't want to reach the academy exhausted after a sleepless night. That was no way to start a new experience.

Still, Moreau. Was she always looking down on Ritchie, or wasn't she? If she wasn't, did she know how she sounded? Maybe she had no idea how snobbish she came across as.

She and Fitz were tight. They had shared a social scene with a seemingly endless list of friends in common.

At least Ritchie wasn't the only one left out. There was Weld. His background, if anything, was even more hard scrabble than hers.

And yet her attempts to be friendly with him weren't gaining much traction. Eating dinner that close to the Lady Fabron for the second night in a row had definitely fouled his mood. He hadn't said a word all through the meal, and in their cabin after, he had only sunk into a deeper stew. He didn't speak to the others even when Ritchie attempted to draw him into the conversation.

Not that she had been able to find many openings into a discussion that constantly looped back to all the parties Moreau had seen Fitz at.

Ritchie sighed, turned onto her other side, and forced her breathing to slow until her heartbeat finally did likewise. She couldn't start life at the academy on the wrong foot. She already had so much stacked against her. She had studied as hard as she could, trained even harder.

What if it ended up not being enough?

To her annoyance, she felt hot tears pricking at the corners of her eyes, threatening to spill. But then she heard voices in the corridor outside their cabin, distraction enough to turn her mind away from her own anxieties.

Who was talking?

She couldn't catch any words, but she was sure the male voice was Feliks. She was less sure about the female voice, but then something in its uplifting tone brought Tassa's rosy face to mind. Well, that made sense. She was the steward of the only other car still attached to the train; of course she was still on board.

Feliks spoke again, sounding worried or anxious or something. When Tassa responded she once more spoke with such an air of reassurance that Ritchie—who couldn't make out any words but knew of course there was no way Tassa could possibly be speaking to her anyway—felt like a weight had lifted off of her own mind.

The two stewards moved away from outside the cabin door, walking in different directions, although from the footsteps, Ritchie couldn't tell who was who.

But now, now she felt like she could sleep.

She was just starting to drift away when she found herself staring wide-eyed into the grayness of the cabin. Something had woken her. The sound of bedding being thrown back.

Fitz was out of his bunk. Ritchie froze, pretending to be asleep as she felt his eyes moving over her.

Then he opened the door, darting quickly into the corridor and closing the door again before anyone else could wake.

The lights in the corridor had been turned down low. Neither Weld nor Moreau stirred. So only Ritchie was awake.

What was Fitz up to? Pacing the halls? As if Shackleton Fitz IV ever laid awake in the thralls of an anxiety attack. He was probably just making a late-night trip to the bathroom.

When he came back a moment later, she was sure that was all it was. But just as she was nearly asleep again, she heard the sound of rustling bedding once more.

Now it was Moreau heading out into the corridor. Fitz must have woken her after all, and being awake, she had decided she might as well head down the hall herself.

A moment later, she was back, and a handful of minutes after that, the soft sound of her snoring once more filled the cabin.

But again, just as Ritchie was about to sink into sweet slumber, she was awakened by the sound of someone moving in the cabin.

Weld. It had to be. There was no one else left.

Ritchie waited for him to go out into the corridor before turning over, putting her back to the cabin and pressing her nose against the wall. Soon enough he would be back, and then the only possible interruption would be her own bladder.

But she had gone before getting into bed in the first place. She would be fine.

Her last thought, as the first whispers of a dream were cascading over her mind, was that Weld had been gone for rather a long time.

This time she woke with such a start, she bolted upright. Or tried to; the bunk didn't have enough space for that, and her forehead impacted with the ceiling hard enough to make her see stars.

"Ritchie?" Fitz asked, sounding more asleep than awake.

"It's nothing," she said, rolling up onto one elbow and probing her forehead for lumps.

"No, something is happening," Moreau said from the bunk below hers. "Someone ran past our room a second ago, and now there goes someone else."

Ritchie looked at Fitz in the bunk across from hers, and she could see him listening. Then she could hear it too: voices and more footsteps.

Then the door was opening, the corridor this time full of bright lights. Weld had opened the door, but from the inside. He had come back into the cabin at some point after Ritchie had fallen asleep, then.

"What's going on?" Weld asked.

"Nothing! Nothing at all! Sorry for the disturbance," someone said to him, but never slowed his steps on his way past.

"Well, that wasn't terribly convincing," Moreau said.

"Let's go check it out," Fitz said.

"But where are they going?" Ritchie said, even as she pulled on her uniform pants and tunic and hopped down to find her boots.

"Back of the train," Weld said, poking his head out into the hall.

Ritchie pretended to be focused on tugging on her left boot, but through her sleep-tousled bangs she studied Weld's face. Something wasn't quite right about it, but what?

He certainly seemed as ignorant as the rest of them. But just where had he gone, and for so long?

Then she realized what was different. The anger that had been simmering in him throughout the evening was gone. He had gone to bed still stewing, but now he looked...

At peace, Ritchie finally decided. He looked like he had found a relief valve for his anger.

"Ritchie?" Fitz asked. He sounded worried, and she wondered what expressions were playing over her own face.

"I'm okay," she said, tugging on her other boot and following the others into the bright light of the corridor. Fitz was still looking at her like he didn't quite believe her, and she could see the question starting to form on his lips, but when she gave him a quick shake of the head, he let it go.

Just like old times. Fitz had changed. He wasn't the same person as the kid she had been best friends with for most of her childhood. But that kid was still there inside him. It hadn't entirely disappeared during that endless succession of posh parties.

"Lights on," Weld said, looking around as he emerged into the corridor. "That's a safety feature. Something's happened. Something major."

"How do you know?" Fitz asked.

"My parents do cleaning, maintenance and repair for the fourth quadrant branch of this same train line," Weld said.

"Interesting," Fitz said. "So when you say something major, you mean like engine failure?"

"Not in the back of the train," Weld said with a shake of his head.

"No, nothing in the back of the train but the observation car," Moreau said.

"The observation car and the VIP car," Fitz said. "This emergency, it must be a passenger. Someone's been hurt."

"Or killed," Weld said.

Ritchie really wished he hadn't just said that out loud.

6

FITZ WAS ABOUT to move out into the corridor when Weld suddenly stepped back, pushing them all back into the cabin.

"Hey, Weld?" Fitz said in as amiable a tone as he could muster.

"Crew," Weld whispered over his shoulder. Then Fitz heard the running footsteps and two crew members raced past. They weren't dressed as stewards. One of them looked like he might actually be the train commander.

"Go on," Fitz said, nudging Weld's back. Weld took the hint and went back out into the overly bright corridor. Fitz and the others followed and, without a word, they all started walking with brisk steps towards the back of the train.

Then Fitz found himself colliding with Weld's wide back again. He couldn't see past Weld to get a clue what the trouble was this time, but before he could ask, he heard the colonel's voice say, "cadets." Like they'd all just happened upon each other while out for a stroll.

"Something is happening, sir," Weld said.

"Well, let's see if we can be of any use," the colonel said, to Fitz's surprise. He had been sure the colonel was just going to herd them back into their cabin. Instead, he led them to the back of the car and into the airlock between cars. He tried the door to the VIP car first, but it wouldn't open for him.

"If the emergency were in that car, all doors would be open," Weld told him. "That's train company protocol."

"Open like that door is?" Fitz asked, pointing to the door that led down to the tunnel to the observation car. It, too, was brightly lit.

The colonel led the way through the narrow space and then back up to the level of the observation car.

The skies pressed down around the windows, rain lashing against the glass with a sound like metal pellets fired from a gun. Fitz saw Ritchie hugging herself as she looked all around with huge eyes, although the environment inside the train was as comfortably warm as ever.

"Are you okay?" he asked.

She looked at him and nodded, but her grip around herself didn't loosen a bit.

"You'll get used to it," Moreau said with something almost like kindness in her voice. "The sky is just huge, isn't it? It goes on forever."

Ritchie nodded again and offered the smallest of smiles. Fitz looked up at the sky again. The storm clouds hung low and heavy, where they could even be seen through all the rain and darkness. The skies on Buennagel had been much more impressive. That blue, that had gone on forever. Had she forgotten?

The train crew members were gathered in a huddle at the back of the car near the last row of chairs before the glass bubble. The colonel had already approached them and was deep in a whispered conversation with the train commander.

"What's going on?" Moreau asked, rising up on tiptoe, which still didn't allow her to see over even Ritchie's shoulder.

Fitz couldn't see past the crowd of blue uniforms either, but apparently Weld could. The red-head's usual peaches and cream complexion had blanched to an ashen gray.

"What is it?" Fitz asked him.

"The Lady Fabron," Weld said, his eyes starting to dart over to Fitz but then darting back without quite making eye contact. "She's dead."

"Dead?" Ritchie whispered. "But how? And why here?"

Fitz stepped out of the aisle to a space between two of the observation chairs and could just make out one of the crew members holding a medical scanner, although all he could see of the Lady Fabron was her knees. She was sitting in one of the chairs, but from the way her skirt was hitched up on one side, she rather looked like she had collapsed into it.

Then the colonel came back to where they were standing, waving with his hands for the others to follow Fitz's lead and not block the aisle.

"What happened to her, sir?" Ritchie asked.

"It seems she had a heart attack," the colonel said. "The train sensors detected it, but it was very quick. She was dead before the first of the medical bots reached her, and they couldn't revive her."

Something slammed, and they all jumped, but it was just the door to the VIP car banging open. Captain Berger stood there, barefoot and with his shirt undone as if he had just gotten out of bed.

"Lady Fabron?" he asked, straining to see around the crew members.

"Dead, I'm afraid," the colonel said. "Heart attack."

To Fitz's surprise, the old captain looked stricken by the news. He blinked repeatedly, although his eyes stayed dry. His hand grasped the back of one of the chairs and then the other quickly followed, as he suddenly needed the support of both to stay on his feet.

"Did you know her well, sir?" Ritchie asked. She put her hand on one of his, clutching the seat back so tightly the knuckles were going white. The captain looked up at her as if he had never seen her species before.

"Not well," he said after a long moment. "Not personally, that is. Her family is revered throughout all of Loindetu and all of its colonies. *She* is revered."

"I am quite sorry for your loss," the train commander said, taking off his cap to rub at his brow. "We will, of course, run thorough diagnostics on all systems when we dock, but the preliminary checks all confirm there was nothing more we could've done. She went very fast."

"You would know if she had any relevant medical history, correct?"

Ritchie said. "It would be required to travel, so that the medical bots would be on alert."

"Yes, that is correct," the train commander said. "She had no such history, but she is of an age where such things are known to happen."

"She should've been traveling with her own medical team," Captain Berger said. "She earned that and more."

"Well, I'm sure you're right," the commander said with the air of someone who is hoping the point will drop out of the conversation before things get awkward.

"Heart attack," Weld muttered under his breath. "She had no heart."

"What's that?" Captain Berger asked, narrowing his eyes.

"Nothing," the colonel said. "She lost her husband as well as all of her sons in the... wars, isn't that right?" he asked.

Fitz just bit back a scoff. He didn't know if the colonel had been about to say "expansion" or "illegal" or what, but he was not as neutral in the matter as he pretended to be.

"Every one," the captain agreed with a solemn nod of his head. "She had her heart broken so many times over." He shot Weld a glare that said he had heard what the cadet said quite clearly.

"Yes, well," the commander said awkwardly. "There is really nothing to be done here. We will take care of the Lady Fabron and see her body delivered to her estate. In the meantime, perhaps you should all just go back to your cabins. If you need anything, a nightcap or something, just ring the stewards."

"Where is her assistant?" Ritchie asked. Her cheeks reddened as the colonel shot her a look for piping up for a second time, but she didn't drop her eyes.

"Yes, where is that fellow?" Captain Berger asked. "Baptiste Rose, was it?"

"Asleep in his cabin, I assume," the train commander said. "Not as light a sleeper as some."

"Is the Felzkinder with him?" Ritchie asked.

"That's actually a very good question," the train commander said and brushed past the captain to reach inside the door to the VIP car. He made a jabbing motion like pressing a call button. Tassa Sokolov appeared at his elbow almost instantly.

"Sir?" she said. "You told me to stay in the car."

"Yes, quite right," the commander said. "Only, where is that creature the lady had with her? It wasn't here in the observation car when the medical alerts went off. Is it still in her cabin? Or with her assistant, perhaps?"

It was very obvious the commander was keen not to have that temper tantrum-throwing creature of mischief roaming loose and unattended throughout his train.

"I'll check," Tassa assured him, but when she spun to head back into the VIP car, she nearly collided with the Lady Fabron's assistant. "My pardon, sir!"

He looked at her as if her words made no sense to him, then looked past her to everyone else packed into the observation car.

"What's going on?" he asked.

"I'm sorry to be the bearer of bad news," the commander said, reaching out to take the man's elbow and pull him into the observation car, then giving Tassa a very pointed look over his shoulder until she snapped to attention and spun to start the Felzkinder hunt.

"What is it?" Mr. Rose asked, craning to see around the crowd. He must have caught a glimpse of something, as his eyes went wide before the commander even began to answer him.

"Your employer, the Lady Fabron, has had a heart attack," the commander said. "It was very sudden. By the time the medical bots reached her from the front of the car, she was beyond saving. I am sorry."

"But why was she even here?" Mr. Rose asked.

"The view?" Fitz hadn't meant to speak out loud, but sometimes he just couldn't help himself. The sound of rain against the glass seemed to grow twice as loud as everyone stared at him.

"Mr. Rose," Ritchie said. "Where is Chou-Chou?"

"Chou-Chou?" he repeated. "He was with me." His voice trailed off as he turned to look back down the corridor behind him. "He *was*."

"He isn't here," Tassa said as she came back down the corridor at a run. "I even checked the unoccupied rooms, even though he'd need to steal a steward key to get inside them. He's definitely not in the VIP car. Should I extend the search, sir?"

"Chou-Chou is missing?" Mr. Rose seemed to be having trouble waking his brain up.

"I know you've had a terrible shock, but you must help us find him," the commander said. "You know him better than any of us, where he might go or hide or what have you. You do understand I can't have such a creature loose on my train."

"No, of course not," Mr. Rose said, but he still looked confused. He turned to Tassa. "Chou-Chou was with me last night. He quite wore me out; I guess I fell asleep before he did. But you saw him with me after dinner, didn't you?"

"Yes, he was with you after dinner," Tassa said. "You came back from the diner car nearly an hour before the Lady Fabron and the captain did."

"Did the Lady come into my room to get Chou-Chou after I fell asleep?" he asked.

"Not that I saw," Tassa said. She shifted her weight from foot to foot, as if debating whether to go on. "I guess Chou-Chou wore you both out last night. She said she needed a little break, a night without him for once."

"And she went to the observation car?" Mr. Rose asked.

"No, she went into her cabin," Tassa said. "That was quite a few hours ago. I didn't see her leave to come here. I don't know how long she was here."

"It doesn't matter," the commander said. "The systems diagnostics will verify the train systems did not fail and we're not culpable for her death. Anything beyond that is surely the deceased lady's business, and we should respect the privacy of even her last moments."

Tassa nodded glumly. Mr. Rose slumped into one of the chairs.

"But the Felzkinder," the commander went on. "That's another matter. It must be found."

Fitz heard Ritchie make a small noise, like she had been about to raise an alarm but had cut it off for fear of raising a false alarm. Then she brushed past him to get back into the aisle, weaving her way through the crew members still clustered around Lady Fabron's body to get to the glass observation bubble.

Captain Berger was offering his expertise in hunting down animals, and the colonel was putting all the cadets at the commander's disposal if he needed more eyes on the search, but Fitz tuned them all out, following Ritchie to the very back of the train.

"You saw something," he said to her as she cupped her hands around her eyes to block out the light.

"Maybe," she said, a long uncertain drawl.

"You saw something," he said again with more confidence. Ritchie didn't make mistakes.

She did, however, have a tendency to hesitate when she should be speaking up.

"What's out there?" he asked her.

"Something," she said. "Something is following the train. Is that possible?"

"Like a ship?" Fitz asked, moving to press his own face against the glass and cup his hands around his eyes.

"No, smaller," Ritchie said. "Don't you see? Just there, bouncing like crazy through the rain. It's small, but there's definitely something there."

"Small like a Felzkinder?" Fitz asked her.

"Maybe," she said, pulling her face away from the glass to look at him. He did the same. He could see it in her eyes. She desperately wanted to be wrong. Because the Felzkinder tumbling along in the antigravity field behind the train was sure to be all kinds of bad news.

"Colonel," Fitz said, pitching his voice to carry the length of the observation car over the voices of the others trying to organize search parties. "Ritchie found the Felzkinder."

7

THE TRAIN CREW FROZE, looking from Fitz to their commander.

Their commander frowned, as if not sure whether or not he should take Fitz seriously.

But Colonel Hansen double-timed down the aisle of the observation car to look through the window between Fitz and Ritchie.

"Where?" he asked.

"There," Ritchie said, trying to point at what she could clearly see despite the sheets of rain and the dark gray light that was only now starting to lighten with the coming dawn.

"I see... something," the colonel said. He watched its bouncing movement for several moments, then turned to the commander. "Cadet Ritchie is correct. Something the size of the Felzkinder is out there, bouncing around at about the point of the last of the antigravity disks. I assume there is no way we picked up a bit of hitchhiking debris from the ground, so it must have come from the train."

"But if anyone opened any of the doors, all manner of alarms would have gone off," the commander said. Even so, he too marched to the back of the train to look out into the darkness. "There is something out there," he said at last, then turned to the nearest member of the train crew. "Call up to the bridge. See if they can see that thing on their sensors."

"Yes, sir!" she said and ran back towards the VIP car.

"Why they haven't already noticed it, I have no idea," the commander muttered under his breath, then glanced up at Ritchie, Fitz and the colonel as if he had forgotten they were standing there right next to him. "We'll get to the bottom of this."

"They've got it, commander," the crew member said from the other end of the car. "They're towing it in."

"Very good. Stand back," the commander said, raising his arms to herd them back towards the chairs. Ritchie took several steps back, only noticing when she was no longer within the observation bubble that the bottom of the floor, which had appeared to be clear glass like the rest of the bubble, just barely showed the outline of a hatch.

Then the colonel stepped in front of her and blocked her view. She tried to lean around him, but the commander was in the way.

"Here," Fitz said close to her ear, guiding her to his other side. She was now looking through two layers of glass, the back of the car and the curvature of the observation bubble both, but it was easier to see through than a human body.

The bouncing object was drawing closer, but its trajectory was very irregular. Fitz nudge her shoulder and pointed down, and she noticed the last of the antigravity disks moving underneath it. She couldn't see the field it was projecting, but its movement matched that of the Felzkinder's body. When the last disk was under the body, the body bounced high, but when the disk lifted off from the ground and raced to the front of the train, the body dropped down until the next disk in line caught it back up again.

"Stand back," the commander said, dropping to one knee beside the hatch. He pressed his hand to what must have been a palm lock, although it was by all appearances more clear glass. There was a flash of green light and a click, and the outlines of the hatch became even more definite.

Then the back of the car was filled with the roar of wind. Ritchie flinched and turned her face away from the sudden onslaught of freezing rain pelting her like little stinging darts. She could hear the commander yelling something and she thought the colonel yelled something back, but their words were completely lost in the shrieks of the wind.

Then the hatch clanged shut again, and all was silent.

Ritchie wiped the cold water from her face, then slicked the wet hair back off her forehead.

"Are you okay?" Fitz asked. His thick hair was still dripping, but he didn't seem to even notice.

"I'm fine," she said. "How's the Felzkinder?"

"Dead, I'm afraid," the commander said. He had the sodden little body in his arms, looking more than ever like a furry infant. He carried it towards the back of the observation car, where one of the crew members was waiting with a thick blanket. The commander pointed his chin towards the floor and the crew member spread out the blanket. Then the commander dropped back to one knee and gently laid the body down on the ground.

It flopped over on its back, chubby arms and legs sprawling everywhere. At first glance, Ritchie thought it was just the wetness from the rain that was darkening its honey-colored fur.

Then she realized it was blood. A lot of blood.

"That's a bad bit of business," Captain Berger said with a tisk of his tongue.

Ritchie crept closer to get a better look. There was a long gash across the Felzkinder's torso, from its left hip up to its right arm pit. It had bled profusely.

"Effective, though," the colonel said.

The captain tisked his disapproval again.

"Well, it's pretty much the opposite of a clean kill," the colonel said. "Was whoever did this trying to torture the poor creature?"

"It didn't die right away?" Ritchie asked. She couldn't take her eyes off that gash. Blood from it had run everywhere, coating the fur so thickly it hadn't washed away even in that storm. And yet, it didn't look like a very deep cut.

"Well, someone would have to do an autopsy to be sure, but my guess would be that animal wasn't even dead yet when it was thrown from the train," he said. "In fact, the cold out there might have even slowed the whole process down."

"*Will* there be an autopsy?" Ritchie asked.

The commander looked surprised at the question. "No. Why would there be?"

"Because this is clearly murder?" Ritchie said, appalled she should even have to point that out.

"Technically, no," Mr. Rose said. He was still collapsed in one of the chairs, hands thrust between his legs so that his face was nearly resting on his knees, and his eyes were filled with tears. "Chou-Chou chose not to be emancipated. Legally, he is a pet, a belonging of the Lady Fabron. All of his paperwork was in order; the law will be quite clear on that point."

"You can't murder a possession," the commander said.

"But, destruction of property, then?" Ritchie asked.

"I don't think that would warrant an autopsy," he said, shaking his head. He gently drew the edges of the blanket around the Felzkinder like a parent swaddling a baby, but the last fold came down over its chubby face and he disappeared from view.

The commander stood up, briefly pressed the bridge of his nose between his thumb and forefinger, then looked up at the colonel. "It's not up to me, of course. This body and the Lady Fabron's will both be turned over to her estate when we reach it; it was already on our itinerary. The estate will decide what happens next. All I know is that the train line is not culpable."

"Who at the estate decides?" Fitz asked. Then, as no one answered, he added, "Mr. Rose?"

"I don't know," he said. The fact that he was speaking towards the floor was probably why his voice seemed to be coming from so far away. "There are lawyers, here and back on Loindetu. They'll tell me what to do."

"You'll have to call them," Fitz said. "They should be informed of what happened here."

"Of course," he said, still speaking towards the floor. "Yes, I must do that."

"She had no heirs," Captain Berger said. "All of her sons died in the war, no grandchildren."

"Mr. Rose, why don't you come with me?" the commander said, putting a hand on the slight man's shoulder. "We can send a priority message through the jump network from the bridge. That will be better than what you can do directly with your implant."

"Yes, of course," Mr. Rose said, still sounding far away. But then he stiffened up, hands closing into fists as his entire body became one tight knot. Just when Ritchie was sure he was going to explode, he relaxed again. Then he sat up straight and looked directly at the commander. "Of course. Thank you."

"Well, no need for search parties now," the colonel said to the four cadets. "Although I doubt any of you are going to be getting any sleep, you might as well head back to your cabin until breakfast."

"Yes, sir," Fitz said for all of them.

They went back through the tunnel to their own sleeper car. The colonel stayed behind in the observation car, exchanging murmurs of words with Captain Berger.

"Our colonel sure seems like a fun guy," Moreau said when they were well beyond the point where she might be overheard. "Imagine knowing so much about how long a knife cut would take to kill you."

"At least he seemed put off by it," Fitz said. "That Captain Berger just seemed sort of disappointed in the attempt. Like he wanted to give whoever murdered that poor thing a bad grade in execution."

"This can't be the end of it," Ritchie said, as Moreau keyed the door to their cabin open and went inside. Weld followed, but Fitz lingered in the corridor with Ritchie.

"What do you mean?" he asked.

"Two people just died in very suspicious circumstances, and no one is investigating anything?" she said.

"Technically, one person died in very mundane circumstances, and one personal possession was destroyed in, admittedly, a very suspicious manner," Fitz said. Then he caught Ritchie's elbow and drew her a little further down the corridor. "It's upsetting. I don't disagree with you there. But we'll be at the academy soon. What can we do?"

Ritchie bit at her lip. She couldn't help glancing past Fitz to where she could see Weld's right shoulder and just a wedge of his face.

Fitz turned to follow her gaze, then looked back at her.

"What are you thinking?" he asked.

"Nothing," Ritchie said.

"You know, you've never been able to lie to me," Fitz said.

"That's not true," Ritchie said. "I think what you mean to say is that I've never tried to lie to you. Whether I could get away with it or not is unproven."

"Fair enough," Fitz said. "Tell me what you're thinking."

Ritchie wanted to. But when she tried to organize her thoughts into actual sentences, she realized what it would all sound like if she said them out loud.

Weld had worked hard for this opportunity, perhaps even harder than she had. And she was going to maybe jeopardize that for him by throwing possibly baseless accusations around?

It didn't matter what she suspected; it only mattered what she could prove.

She didn't know where he had gone the night before when he had left the cabin. She didn't even know how long he was gone. All she had was a sense that he had been angry when he left, and at peace when they all woke up later.

Maybe just a few hours of sleep had taken the edge off his anger. He had been angry the night before after watching the Lady Fabron in the formal dining room, and that had dissipated on its own. So why not a second time?

"Ritchie?" Fitz said.

"It's nothing," she said, but the narrowing of his eyes told her he didn't really believe her. She mustered up a smile and tried for an upbeat tone. "Really, it's nothing. And we're probably worried about nothing. Mr. Rose is calling the attorneys now, and do you really think someone like Lady Fabron hired attorneys who wouldn't relish any kind of fight on her behalf? And what about the colonel? He stayed behind just now. For all we know, he's trying to figure out what happened too. It probably seemed to us like no one cared because no one is going to let a bunch of kids know what they're really planning to do about anything. Right?"

"If you say so," Fitz said.

"I do," Ritchie said. "I believe it. It's all going to be fine. And the train stops at Lady Fabron's estate before it takes us on to the academy, so we'll know how this all turns out in the end."

"You sound very sure," Fitz said.

"I am," she said. "Now, if you'll excuse me, I have a ton more reading to get through before we get to the academy."

"Yeah," Fitz said. "I guess I do too."

She brushed past him to head into the cabin, and he followed behind. She took out her tablet and paged through the files until she found something to look at.

She had read all the assignments already, proof positive that she was completely capable of lying to Fitz. But she forced her eyes to track the text as if reading it for the first time. She could feel Fitz watching her, not even pretending to look at his own reader.

She wished he would look away, but only because she wanted to be the one pretending to read while she secretly studied the cadet next to her.

She had been sneaking peeks at Weld all morning, and his face never changed. It was stony, impassive, perhaps a shade too pale. But it had never changed.

Since meeting him, the strongest impression she had of him was how on the surface his feelings were. He had strong reactions to Moreau when they met, to Ritchie when he realized who she was, to Fitz and his history of failing up.

Not to mention his reaction to the mere sight of Lady Fabron and Chou-Chou.

But his hated foe's sudden death left him stoically feeling nothing? No, Ritchie didn't believe that, not for one minute.

Perhaps he was just keeping himself bottled tight because being demonstrably celebratory at a tragic death would be beyond improper. Perhaps he was being mindful of the uniform he wore and the demeanor he was meant to convey while wearing it, especially after all that had been said after that disastrous dinner.

Perhaps that's all it was. She had no real proof otherwise.

Not to mention, even when she called back the image of him at his most angry, she still couldn't imagine him doing what had been done to that Felzkinder.

Still, she was glad there were two other cadets in the cabin with her. Even if the three of them together were barely a match in size for one Weld.

8

FITZ SAT with his reader on his lap, not even bothering to look at it.

Ritchie wasn't telling him something.

On one level, he couldn't blame her. He had given her no reason to believe he was any more reliable than when they were kids. Why *would* she confide in him?

And yet, somehow, he didn't think this was about him. This was like her seeing the Felzkinder bouncing along behind the train and not saying a word. What had happened to her confidence? She hadn't trusted her own eyesight. What sense was she not trusting now?

Ritchie wasn't studying either, although Fitz knew she was making a better show of it than he was. She kept her eyes scanning and her finger swiping through pages at a steady rhythm, but her actual attention was on something else.

She had a suspicion she wasn't sharing with him. Fine.

He had suspicions, too.

The colonel had sounded both knowledgeable and confident in his assessment that the Felzkinder had not yet been dead when it had been tossed out of the train. What if Lady Fabron's heart attack was because she had seen her beloved pet bleeding to death out in that storm? Then the one death had caused the other. It made sense.

But what would Lady Fabron have been doing in the observation car all alone in the first place?

Fitz tossed his reader aside with a sigh and got up. "I'm going for a walk," he announced.

"I thought the colonel wanted us to stay here?" Ritchie said tentatively.

"Well, I'm not good at sitting still," Fitz said. "I'm just going to stretch my legs a bit. If he comes looking for me, give a shout. I won't be far."

Moreau nodded without looking up from her reader. Weld narrowed his eyes and studied Fitz's face as if searching for clues of a lie, but in the end just shrugged and turned his attention back to his own reader.

"Don't get in trouble," Ritchie said. "It'll look bad on the rest of us, you know."

"I know," Fitz said. That lesson he had learned at his last school, and the memory of it still stung. "I'll just be in the corridor."

He slipped out of the cabin and closed the door behind him.

The door at the end of the car was still standing open, as was the door beyond that led down to the tunnel. Surely the bodies had been moved by now? So why were the emergency protocols still in effect?

On a whim, he touched the door that led into the VIP car. It shouldn't open to him, as he didn't have the correct access. But to his surprise, it did. He stepped into the corridor with carpet that was just a touch lusher than the one in the last car, the lighting a touch warmer, the fixtures a touch posher.

He heard a sniffling sound and followed it to a tiny alcove off the main corridor. It had no door, so it wasn't one of the cabins. The walls around him were nothing but cabinets with doors of a dizzying array of sizes, and as he turned the corner, he found the source of the sound.

Tassa Sokolov jumped as she sensed him in her space and turned to face him, scrubbing tears from her cheeks.

"Did you need something?" she asked, her voice as politely cheery as ever despite the red tinge to her eyes. "Are you looking for Feliks?"

"No, I just notice the door was open," he said, pointing a thumb back over his shoulder as if she might not know which door he meant. "Are you all right?"

"Oh, yes," she said. "The doors are open because the bridge crew keeps passing through. It was easier than conducting them through each time. Not that I have more important work to be doing at the moment." She looked around at the cabinet doors but didn't move to open any of them.

"I'm sure this must be very upsetting for you," Fitz said. "You just lost half your passengers at once."

"I did," she said, and fresh tears welled at the corners of her eyes. "I know Feliks would say I was being silly. They're just passengers, not family."

"I think that's probably why Feliks is still the steward on our end while you've been assigned the VIP car," Fitz said. "You genuinely care. Someone like the Lady Fabron can tell the difference between sincerity like that and someone who's just sucking up to the rich clients."

"That's true," Tassa said. "She was demanding, but she was fair. And she had such a sadness about her. Did you see her eyes? She had such sad eyes."

"I didn't get a close look at her," he admitted. "But I've heard a bit of her history."

"Yes," Tassa said. "And she really loved her Chou-Chou. I guess the one good thing to come out of this is that she died before she saw what had become of him."

"Er." Fitz decided not to argue that point. "Chou-Chou seemed like he would have been a challenge for you as a steward as well. He was quite upset that last night."

"Yes, and it took quite a while to settle him down," Tassa said. "He has a sweet tooth, but he can't have sweets. He's old for a Felzkinder and has a very restrictive diet. Not that you can explain something like that to a Felzkinder."

"Did Mr. Rose call you for help?" Fitz asked.

"Yes. I replicated some of the foods he likes... liked that he could have," she said. The switch to the past tense put a hitch in her voice. She gestured to the replicator built into the wall behind her. "We tried everything we could think of. In the end, I think he just cried until exhaustion took him."

"Feliks said there were no in-cabin replicators, not even in the VIP car," Fitz said.

"That's right," Tassa said. "It's part of the train line's full-service experience."

"And if someone needs something in the middle of the night?" Fitz asked.

"I get up and get it," she said. "I stay in uniform and on call the entire trip. Then I get a few days off before the next trip out."

"That sounds positively exhausting," Fitz said.

"Really? I would've thought being a soldier was more demanding," she said.

"I haven't declared for a branch yet," Fitz said.

"I don't think diplomats have an easier time of it than guardians," Tassa said. Then she blushed. "I applied to the academies every year I was eligible. I never got accepted, but I wished for it so hard. I admit I'm envious of the four of you."

"We did just take the last four slots," Fitz said. "Of course, we all might still wash out before university."

"I hope not!" Tassa said. "Just work hard. You're almost there."

"Well, *I* intend to," he said. Then he let the smile drop from his face, his tone all serious again. "Say, do you have any idea why the Lady Fabron was alone in the observation car last night?"

"No," Tassa said. "She was very late coming back from dinner, I remember that. I gathered that she and the captain had retired to the saloon after the meal." She lowered her voice conspiratorially. "She was a bit tipsy when she came back. Actually friendly and so funny! It was like getting a glimpse of what she must have been like at our age. You know, before all the tragedy."

"She and the captain were drinking together?" Fitz asked, also adopting a conspiratorial tone.

"Well, yes, but she came back alone," Tassa said. "So it wasn't anything, you know, like *that*. I think Chou-Chou being out of sorts was upsetting her, and that's why she lingered over dinner rather than coming back to deal with him. I offered to fetch him from Mr.

Rose's cabin, but she said not to bother. For one night she could sleep alone."

"Maybe she couldn't," Fitz said. "Maybe she was too lonely without him and that's why she got up in the middle of the night."

"Maybe, but if she was looking for Chou-Chou, she would've woken Mr. Rose first, and she didn't," Tassa said.

"Did you know she was up?" Fitz asked.

"No, she didn't ring for me," Tassa said. "It was late, long past dinner, and I sleep when I can."

"You must sleep light," Fitz said.

"I do," Tassa said. "I sleep here, actually. That panel there folds down into my hammock, which hooks over there."

"If she had left her cabin to go to the front of the train, you would've heard her pass," Fitz guessed.

"Yes," Tassa said.

Then, as if to prove her point, they both heard footsteps in the corridor. Someone was walking softly, but even those muffled sounds seemed to echo through the doorless alcove.

"A crew member," Tassa said to Fitz.

"You're sure?" he asked. There was a soft knock, the swish of a door opening, and then a low voice speaking what sounded like a greeting.

"Yes, someone is talking to Mr. Rose," she said. "Perhaps there was a response from the lady's lawyers." The door hissed shut again, and the silence returned, broken only by the barely discernible sound of the rain outside the train. "So, yes, I would've heard her pass," Tassa said. "Or if she'd knocked on Mr. Rose's door looking for Chou-Chou, I would've heard that. His cabin is the first one on the left."

"So she just quietly slipped out of her cabin and went to the back of the train," Fitz said.

"I think so," Tassa said. "Maybe she just wanted to look out at the storm."

"That does seem the most likely thing," Fitz said. "Do you know who found her body?"

"Do you mean the first person?" Tassa asked. "That was me. The alarms went off all over the train, but as I was the closest of the stewards, I was the first one there."

"I'm sorry," Fitz said, catching her hand to give it a reassuring squeeze.

"It was awful," she said. "The medical bots were all over her, but there was nothing they could do."

"The bots sensed when her heart stopped?" he asked.

"I guess," Tassa said. "They're supposed to notice a lot more than that. For instance, in the saloon cars, they monitor blood alcohol levels and compare that to species norms, so the bartenders know when to stop serving a particular passenger. Also, food allergies in the dining areas, people getting sick alone in their cabins, things like that."

"The commander said she must have died suddenly," Fitz said.

Fresh tears flooded Tassa's eyes. "She was still warm when I touched her. I almost thought it must be a glitch in the systems. She looked warm and alive, you know? She couldn't possibly be dead. Only I could feel something was different. Her spirit was gone, I guess."

"Was she in her nightclothes?" Fitz asked.

Tassa frowned. "No, she was dressed."

"The same as the night before?"

"No, a different outfit. I hadn't even noticed at the time, but thinking back, yes, it was a different outfit," she said. She gave Fitz a puzzled look. "What does that mean?"

"Probably nothing," he said with a smile. "I'm sorry, but can I ask you one more indelicate question?"

"Why are you asking any questions?" Tassa countered. "This really isn't your business."

"To be honest, I just want to understand what happened to her," Fitz said. "I've studied a bit about her life, and this just doesn't feel like how it all should've ended. I'm trying to make it make sense, I guess."

"Knowing what she was wearing helps you with that?" she asked.

"Actually yes," he said. "You admired her, right? She was a tough lady and not easy to like, but she had a quality." Tassa nodded, but there was still a hint of suspicion in her eyes. "Personally, I take comfort in the fact that maybe she felt her end was coming. And she got up and dressed herself as she saw fit and went to have one last look at her adopted homeworld before meeting her end."

"Do you really think that's what happened?" she asked.

No, Fitz thought. *Not remotely.*

"I think that would be an end that would fit with the rest of her life," he said instead.

"I think so too," Tassa said, wiping at her eyes with the air of someone who was all done crying. "What was your last question?"

"It might be upsetting," he warned.

"Go ahead. I'm okay now."

"I didn't really get a good look at the floor of the observation car before we pulled Chou-Chou back inside," Fitz said. "But if he had been in there before the Lady Fabron, there might have been some sort of clue on the carpet, perhaps?"

Like copious amounts of blood, for instance.

"No, I didn't notice anything," Tassa said. "But that couldn't possibly be where he was pushed out of the train."

"Couldn't it?" Fitz said. "He was bouncing along behind; I assumed he had to have been pushed from the back."

"No, I don't think so," she said. "I don't really understand how the antigravity disks work, but I think wherever he had been pushed out of the train, he would've kept bouncing back until he was as far behind the train as he could go. Then he would just be... stuck."

"Oh," Fitz said, making a mental note to research more about how antigravity trains worked. Did no one who worked on one know the slightest bit about it? They all just took it for granted it would work the way it was meant to and left it at that? Maybe he could find someone who worked maintenance. An engineer or something.

"But you saw how wet everything got when they pulled Chou-Chou back in," Tassa said. "If he had gone out the same hatch, I suppose pushing out would be faster than pulling in, but still the carpet would have been soaked with rain. When I got there, it was all perfectly dry."

"So Chou-Chou could've been thrown from any point on the train?" Fitz asked.

"By someone who could open a hatch or airlock," Tassa said. "But those are all set to alarm if opened when the train is moving, and no such alarms went off."

"And nobody thinks that's weird?" Fitz asked.

"*Everybody* thinks it's weird," Tassa said, dropping her voice down to a whisper. "Something is clearly off with the security systems. The entire train is already scheduled for a thorough diagnostic and overhaul because of the medical bots, so no one is saying anymore out loud. But I can tell finding something outside of the train that shouldn't be there is freaking out the bridge crew. A lot."

"But no one really cares about Chou-Chou," Fitz said.

"I care," Tassa said. "I loved that little baby. He was so sweet, when he wasn't all keyed up, desperate for sugary treats. He drew me pictures and gave me little gifts every time he saw me. But the simple fact is, he's considered property."

"And his death, property damage," Fitz said.

"And lesser property damage than whatever was done to the train to hide any evidence of opening a hatch," Tassa said. "Believe me, that's what the train line is most concerned about. And can you blame them? What if it had happened when we were still out in space?"

Fitz shuddered. There was a thought he never wanted to entertain.

9

NOT FOR A MINUTE did Ritchie believe that Fitz was only going out to stretch his legs.

He was up to something. But what?

It was ironic, now that she was free to study Weld as closely as she liked, all of her thoughts were on Fitz and what he was up to.

And yet, Weld looked perfectly normal. If he had a guilty conscience about anything, he hid it very well. Occasionally his brow would furrow, but that was always followed by a tap at his reader screen as he consulted some other text or looked up a word or something. Like all of his attention was focused on his studies, as hers ought to be.

It was hard to tell how engrossed Moreau was in her own reading. She was slouched back in her seat, one long lock of hair pulled free from her topknot so that she could twist it around and around her finger. She didn't look like she was studying so much as she was daydreaming.

"If you're worried about Fitz, perhaps you should go find him," Moreau said without looking up from her reader screen or pausing the twisting of her hair.

Weld did look up and seemed to notice for the first time there were only three of them in the cabin.

"I'm sure he's doing exactly what he said he was doing," Ritchie said.

"That's because you're very trusting," Moreau said. "But you weren't wrong before. If the colonel finds one of us gone, we're all going to get dressed down for it. Maybe not the best way to start our time at the academy."

Weld was starting to look seriously worried.

"She's exaggerating," Ritchie told him. "It'll be fine."

"Maybe I should bring him back here," Weld said and started to set his reader aside.

"No, I'll do it," Ritchie said. "I've finished the reading, anyway. I was just looking it over again to pass the time. I'll find him."

"Okay," Weld said, turning his reader back on before shooting her a look of deep gratitude. "Ritchie, thanks. We worked hard to get this far, didn't we? We can't let one cadet who doesn't care ruin it for us."

"He won't," Ritchie promised, tucking her reader back in her bag. "I'm sure he's just upset about what happened in the observation car."

"You think he's upset?" Weld said skeptically.

"Yes," Ritchie said. "We've known each other since we were kids. I can tell when he's feeling something, even if he doesn't want to show it. That's probably why he wanted a moment alone."

"Lots of people do that," Weld said, scrubbing a fingertip over some blemish on the corner of his reader, not looking at her.

"Do what?" Ritchie asked.

"Hide their feelings," Weld said.

Moreau snorted.

"What?" he asked.

"You show everything, my friend," she said.

"I know I have a fast temper," he said, the tips of his ears going red. But Ritchie could tell he was in that moment embarrassed, not angry. "I cool off fast too." His blush deepened, but he forced the next words out. "I learned some meditation techniques that help. I can calm myself down."

"This comes up a lot, does it?" Moreau asked.

"Moreau, stop teasing him," Ritchie said. "Can't you see he means it?"

Moreau looked at Weld more directly than she had since they had been introduced. "I suppose he does," she said with something like respect.

"This isn't how I wanted to start my academic career, you know," Weld said. "I work hard to control my temper, but that woman. If you knew all she did."

"It's a bit much to ask you to take being in her company in stride, I agree," Ritchie said.

"But I controlled myself," Weld said. "I didn't do half the things I was thinking of while sitting three chairs down from her at dinner."

"We're not judging you," Ritchie said. Then she gave Moreau a hard glare until she murmured her agreement.

"It's just, Fitz isn't the only one upset about what happened," Weld said. "I mean, the lady Fabron got less than she deserved, but that animal didn't ask for any of it. I get that it's sad."

Ritchie nodded. She wanted to believe him, and yet her gut was still telling her there was something off about Weld.

"I'm going to find Fitz," she said instead, and the other two went back to their reading as she left the cabin.

As much as Fitz had implied he would be walking for the sake of walking, she was sure he had headed to the back of the train. She would start there herself.

Although she had no idea if the colonel was inside his cabin or not, she found herself creeping sneakily past his door.

This was no way to start life at the academy, she knew that. If she got caught sneaking around, poking into things that technically weren't any of her business, she would likely get into trouble. Maybe a lot of trouble.

But there was just no way she could leave it alone.

She was about to head towards the tunnel door when she noticed the door to the VIP car was standing ajar. Had Fitz gone that way?

Even if he hadn't, could there be clues inside about what had happened to Lady Fabron or to Chou-Chou?

Ritchie crept closer and listened at the gap of the door. She could hear voices: Fitz and Tassa Sekolov. She gently eased the door a bit further open until she could see down the length of the corridor, but there was no one in sight. Every door appeared to be closed, but there was a very narrow hallway just at the beginning of the corridor, a storage area to judge by the numerous cabinet doors.

If Fitz had come looking to talk to Tassa, that was probably where he had found her. But why had he come looking for Tassa? He hadn't seemed to notice all the shy smiles Tassa had been throwing his way every time they were in the same room together.

Anyway, she had told everyone all she knew while they were all standing in the observation car.

No, if there was anyone who hadn't told their whole story, it was the Lady Fabron's assistant, Mr. Rose.

Her feet were propelling her down the corridor before she even realized she had made a decision. She knocked softly on the first door she came to and bit her lip as she hoped for the best.

When there was no answer, she touched the knob and found she could turn it. Another door left unlocked. She slid it open and just had a glimpse of a rather posher cabin than the one the cadets shared. No one was inside, although it looked like someone had been there quite recently. The pillows on the seats were askew, and a lap blanket lay in a twisted nest on the floor. A plate was next to the blanket, as if someone had been enjoying a snack while curled up warmly.

A messy someone, to judge by the crumbs scattered not just over the plate but all over the carpet, all around it.

Ritchie was just about to step inside when she heard a click and the next door down the corridor opened. Mr. Rose stuck his head out into the corridor. He looked confused until his sweeping gaze finally reached her.

"Are you looking for me?" he asked.

"Yes, I am," she said, closing the door in front of her and walking towards him as quickly as she dared. She expected Tassa and Fitz to burst out into the corridor at any moment and demand she explain what she was up to.

What *was* she up to?

"Did the train commander send you?" Mr. Rose asked when she had reached him.

"No, I just wanted to ask you a few questions. Can we go inside and sit down?"

"Yes, of course," he said, but then stopped abruptly in the doorway so that she was stuck in the corridor. For a minute she thought he had grown suddenly suspicious and changed his mind about talking to her, but he was only looking over his cabin as if to be sure nothing untoward had been left lying about before letting her in.

"I'm sorry I can't offer you anything," he said as he motioned for her to take the chair opposite of him. "There are no replicators in the cabins on this train line, not even on the VIP car."

"So I've been told," Ritchie said. Then she went out on a limb. "Any idea why?"

"Oh," Mr. Rose said, surprised at the question. "Well, I believe the official word is that asking the stewards to fetch things for you rather than getting it yourself is part of the full-service experience. I admit it doesn't make a lot of sense, but that's what they've always told me."

"Yes, I believe I've heard the same," Ritchie said.

"But if you need anything, I can ring—" He gestured towards the call button by the door.

"No, I'm fine," Ritchie said before he quite touched the button. "Really, I only wanted to ask you a few questions about Chou-Chou."

"Chou-Chou," Mr. Rose said, and the rigid posture he had been maintaining all through the formalities of inviting her into his cabin crumpled as if beneath a great weight.

"I'm sorry, I truly don't mean to upset you," Ritchie said. "It just feels so unfair to me to treat him as just property."

"I agree," Mr. Rose said. "Even though it was what he wanted. Both the Lady Fabron and I explained everything to him over and over again before we let him sign the papers that kept him in our care. You *have* to understand that. Legally, he might be considered as a pet, but that's never how we saw him."

"More like a child?" Ritchie asked.

"No, not like a child," Mr. Rose sighed. "Lady Fabron had far too many children to confuse one sort of relationship for another. Perhaps one would have to raise and live with a Felzkinder to know the bond. It's not like a child or a pet. It's a different sort of companion. But the bond is just as strong. Maybe in some ways stronger. Felzkinder don't grow up and get lives of their own like children do, and they live much longer than most pets. Chou-Chou was a special part of our family."

"At least you had one last special moment together, just the two of you. He slept here with you last night, didn't he? Even though he usually slept with the Lady Fabron?" Ritchie asked.

"That's true, but it's not unusual for Chou-Chou to settle in with me at first and then go with the Lady Fabron when she is ready to turn in," Mr. Rose said. "Sometimes social engagements keep her up rather late."

Ritchie wondered how many social engagements an exile on such a remote world could have, but decided that was too far off the main topic. "It must have been hard getting him to settle down last night," she said instead.

"It's not the worst that I've seen him, but it was a challenge," he agreed. "If you can get him distracted with something else, he'll sort himself out. He likes to draw, for instance, and he adores music. Between the two of those things, he calmed down, and we both fell asleep only a little later than usual." He sighed and rubbed tiredly at his own face, and she suspected it had not been so easy as all that.

"You must have slept quite soundly after such a trying evening," Ritchie said.

"Yes, perhaps too soundly," he said softly. "When I woke up, they were both gone. It was only all the voices in the observation car that woke me. Not the Lady Fabron heading to bed, or Chou-Chou sneaking out of the room."

"Can he do that? Get out of the room on his own?" Ritchie asked.

"I wouldn't have thought so, and yet here we are. What other explanation is there?"

"Someone took him?" Ritchie suggested.

"But who would do such a thing? And why?"

"There aren't very many people on the train," Ritchie said carefully.

"Yes," Mr. Rose said, jumping to a conclusion not remotely what she had meant, "it must have been some sort of accident."

"You think he did that to himself?" Ritchie asked.

"Don't we have to think that? The alternative is so very unlikely," he said.

Ritchie studied his face carefully. She saw no hint that he was trying to fool her. He seemed heartbreakingly sincere. Was such an improbable accident actually easier for him to accept than the fact that some person for whatever foul motive had purposely destroyed his cherished companion?

"Could Chou-Chou really do such a thing?" she asked.

"Well, I've seen him do things I never thought he could when the sugar cravings were high in him," Mr. Rose said, studying his own interlaced fingers. "He can get into things, climbing cabinets or opening locks, that sort of thing. Normally, he's not so strong or dexterous or clever. But when the cravings are on him..." He ended with a shrug.

"It's like a drug for him?" Ritchie asked. She had known a few addicts in her old neighborhood. Not well, obviously. But she knew who they were so she could steer clear of them. Over the years, she had seen them break all sorts of boundaries. But those had been more legal and moral boundaries. She had never seen them get enhanced physical abilities or suddenly become super clever.

But to be fair, she knew very little about Felzkinder.

"No, not like that," Mr. Rose said. "Chou-Chou is the sweetest of creatures. Not an addict. But he does have a fondness for sweets. Sadly, as he's gotten older, we've had to add more restrictions to his diet. Blood-cherry cake is the worst. He always throws a tantrum over that one."

"But why? I mean, it sounded like the Lady Fabron eats it quite often."

"She eats blood-cherries often, but usually fresh with cream and in the morning when Chou-Chou is considerably less food-focused," Mr. Rose said. "It's not the blood-cherries he's after, anyway. It's the cake. But it's the blood-cherries that are toxic to his system, you see. He can't have those at all."

"It sounds like a lot of work, caring for him," Ritchie said. She realized too late she was using the present tense, but Mr. Rose didn't seem to notice.

"It's rewarding," he said with a sad smile. "My whole life, caring for the Fabron family, has always been rewarding."

"Lady Fabron was a bit like a mother to you, wasn't she?" Ritchie said.

"I don't remember my real mother," he said, looking out the window at the gray clouds of Oymyakon. The rain was lightening up, although Ritchie suspected it never entirely stopped. "Lady Fabron was all I ever had."

"You were from one of the colonized worlds," Ritchie guessed. "And you even know which one. Were you never tempted to go back home?"

"No," Mr. Rose said. "I know what you must be thinking, and I suppose most people would go back and try to find their own kin. But to me, the Fabron family was my family."

Ritchie said nothing. She didn't doubt his own feelings, she just doubted that those feelings had ever been reciprocated. Lady Fabron had not acted like a woman who thought of Baptiste Rose as her own son. Chou-Chou had been closer to that as far as Ritchie could see.

"I was with the admiral the day he died," Mr. Rose went on. "We were on another colony, and he was assassinated. Most cowardly; he was poisoned at a state dinner honoring the former leader of that planet's resistance, who has about to be made vice governor of the new colony. It took days for him to die. The medical bots couldn't save him."

"I'm sorry you went through that," Ritchie said. "And now you've lost his wife, too."

"I was the one who brought her the news of his death," Mr. Rose went on as if she hadn't spoken. "She was shattered. Just shattered. But she picked herself up and put herself back together, only to have her oldest boy die from a sniper's rifle. And then the next, and the next. I don't know how she lived through it all."

"I'm guessing you were a part of that," Ritchie said. He finally looked away from the window to give her the saddest of smiles.

"I like to think so," he said. "But I don't know if that's true. All I know is from the day I returned after her husband died, I have never left her side. And if she had lived for all the rest of my days, I never would have."

"So, what will you do now?" Ritchie asked.

"I've already contacted the lawyers. The rest is really up to them," Mr. Rose said. "I suppose I'll have to leave the estate now. Find some other place to live, perhaps some other family to serve."

"I'm sure she thought of you in her will," Ritchie said. "She will have taken care of you."

"Actually, I have no idea what is stated in her will now," he said. "I've never given it much thought. After the last of her sons passed, she was going to leave everything to Chou-Chou."

"Chou-Chou? Can he inherit?" Ritchie asked.

"At one time that was possible, when his personhood was a legal gray area. But after he declined emancipation, that was no longer in any way gray," Mr. Rose said. "In both cases, I was to be his paid guardian."

"So, who gets the estate now?" Ritchie asked.

A pained look crossed Mr. Rose's face, and he pressed a shaking hand to his forehead. "I really don't know. I don't want to think about it, not right now. I am sorry, but I don't think I can answer any more of your questions at this time. If you will excuse me?"

She sensed he wanted to go on with some reason she had to go, but the words wouldn't come. But she could see when someone needed a moment alone to grieve in private. She had lived with that feeling for years herself.

"Yes, of course," Ritchie said. "My condolences, Mr. Rose. For both of your losses."

"Thank you," he said.

The moment the door clicked shut, she heard the first of what would surely be many sobs.

10

FITZ HAD EXPECTED to find the observation car blocked off in some way, but instead he found it empty and looking exactly as it had before anything had ever happened there. The bodies were gone, the carpet was clean and dry, and all the chairs were locked in their upright positions.

He walked back to the bubble and looked out at the gloomy landscape, the craggy gaps between mountains that defied being called "valleys."

He found himself looking out over the last of the antigravity disks as if thinking he might find another clue bouncing out there, never catching up with the train.

He sighed and collapsed into the last of the chairs, then got up and moved one seat over as he realized he had been sitting just where the Lady Fabron had died.

The moment his weight came to a rest, the chair underneath him tilted back, giving him a view of the scurrying clouds overhead. It was like the atmosphere was trying to hypnotize him.

"Oh."

At that soft breath of a word, Fitz sat up and looked back to the door to the VIP car. Ritchie was there, but she was already turning back towards the corridor, as if not to disturb him.

"Ritchie," he called. "Come on in. You're not interrupting anything. I was just thinking."

She still hesitated, her hand on the doorframe. But then she turned back and came down the center aisle to sit down on the seat next to him.

"It's like nothing ever happened here," she said.

"And yet, that's not as comforting as I would have thought," Fitz said. She nodded in agreement.

"It's everyone, I think," she said slowly, as if carefully choosing her words. "The whole train. They want everything to be like nothing ever happened, and they want it as soon as possible."

"I suppose creating that illusion is part of their jobs," Fitz said. "This can't be the first time an old passenger has died on the journey."

"No, I suppose not," Ritchie said, but she sounded even more glum than before. Then again, perhaps that was just because she was talking with her chin on her hand and it was muffling her words.

"You're thinking of the Felzkinder," he guessed. "Poor thing."

"I was just talking with Mr. Rose," she said. "He doesn't want to even think about who might have done such a thing."

"No, I don't imagine he would," Fitz said.

"No," she said, sitting up straight and turning to look right at him. "It's not just that he doesn't want to think about it. Who could blame him for that? No, it's that he can't even conceive of the idea. Fitz, he's convinced himself that Chou-Chou did that to himself."

"That's ridiculous," Fitz said, but he could see that she wasn't joking. "Is he in shock?"

"I think so," Ritchie said. "But it makes me so sad. The one person on the train that should be advocating for poor Chou-Chou, and he's already decided he knows all he needs to know."

"Someone on this train is about to get away with a terrible thing," Fitz agreed.

"I don't know," Ritchie said, slumping back into her chair again, this time with her chin in both of her hands. "Maybe he's right. The colonel did say it was very badly done. Maybe he did do it to himself."

"I don't think that's likely," Fitz said.

"The angle of the wound," Ritchie said, half-closing her eyes as she pictured it. "Chou-Chou could have done it. And if he could have, that may be all the proof anyone in charge needs."

"I don't think he did," Fitz said. "I don't think you think so, either."

"No," Ritchie admitted. "But we'll be at the academy soon. We don't have much time to get to the bottom of anything, even if we wanted to. And besides, we were both already breaking the rules by being in the VIP car. If we get into trouble, we get Moreau and Weld into trouble as well. Maybe we should just drop it."

"I don't want to drop it," Fitz said. "Besides, I don't think we should. I think there's something more going on here than just a murdered Felzkinder."

"You mean Lady Fabron?" Ritchie asked. "I thought she had never gone to fetch Chou-Chou last night. Mr. Rose didn't think she had."

"No, Tassa, the VIP steward, said she didn't," Fitz said.

"What else did Tassa say?" Ritchie asked. Fitz would swear it sounded like she was implying something about him and Tassa, only he knew that Ritchie never implied things. She said them straight out.

Or at least the Ritchie he knew always had.

"Whoever threw the Felzkinder out of the train did it without setting off any of the security alarms," Fitz said.

"Oh," Ritchie said, sitting up again.

"Yeah," Fitz said. "Imagine if that happened while we were in space."

"But the train people must care about that," she said.

"Oh, they do," Fitz said. "But they aren't going to look at it in the context of everything else. It'll just be a security systems issue. Someone will fix the glitch or whatever. And yeah, that's important. No one wants anyone to be able to just open doors while the train is in deep space. But think about it. It narrows our list of suspects quite a bit, doesn't it?"

"You think it was a train crew member?" Ritchie asked.

"Or someone who's really good at circumventing security proto-cols," Fitz said.

"But why would anyone like that want to hurt a Felzkinder?"

Ritchie asked. "I mean, the people most likely to be irritated by him are the stewards and waitstaff, not anyone in the technical part of the crew."

"Maybe it was a team effort," Fitz said. "One person lost it with the Felzkinder and the other helped the first one get rid of the evidence."

"Get rid of the body," Ritchie said, then sat up even straighter. "Fitz, there wasn't a knife."

"Maybe it was too small for the antigravity disks to keep up in the air," Fitz said. "It could be anywhere over kilometers of countryside no one is going to want to search," he added, waving a hand towards the passing view.

"Or maybe it's still on the train," she said. Then, "oh!" And he was pretty sure her body couldn't really be described as sitting anymore. More like hovering with minimum contact with the cushion beneath her.

"What?" he asked.

"I saw something," she said. "Come with me."

Then she was up and running back to the VIP car. His chair was still in recline mode and it took him a moment to wrestle back out of it before he could follow.

He found her in the VIP car corridor, standing in the doorway to one of the cabins.

"Whose is this?" he asked as he peaked in over her shoulder. "I would've thought the lady would want more space."

"I don't think anyone was using this one, technically," she said. "You could ask your friend Tassa, though."

Fitz could only see the tops of the seats from around Ritchie. There were no top bunks in this cabin, just some sort of bronze thing he took to be an attempt at art.

"Well?" he said.

"Yeah," Ritchie said and took a step into the cabin. She walked carefully around the edges of the space, and as she circled, he saw the pillows in disarray on the bench seat and a blanket wrapped around like a nest on the floor.

And next to the blanket, a plate strewn with crumbs.

"That's not the platter from dinner last night," he said.

"No," Ritchie said, leaning down to get a closer look without touching anything. "The platter was much bigger, but the plates we ate from were much smaller. This is something different."

"But still cake," Fitz said, squinting at the crumbs.

"Cherry," Ritchie said, pointing to a pinkish smear at the edge of the plate.

"Not blood-cherry, I don't think," Fitz said. "Those were much redder."

"Agreed," Ritchie said.

Then they heard Tassa's voice coming from the end of the corridor, where her alcove was. At first she was muttering to herself, "what's this door doing open?" Then she was in the doorway and saw them both inside the room. "Oh, no. This won't do," she said. It took a bit of work, but she managed to contort her rosy, rounded face into a rather cross expression. "Out."

"Whose room is this?" Ritchie asked, even as Fitz hastened to follow Tassa's command.

"This room? No one," Tassa said, her eyes darting to the side as she momentarily consulted a list only she could see. "No, it's not in use this leg of the journey."

"Well, clearly it's been in use," Ritchie said, sweeping her hands over the blanket, plate, and mess of crumbs.

"You two didn't do this?" Tassa demanded.

"We found it like this," Fitz said.

"How could we do this?" Ritchie asked. "Where would we even get the plate and, I'm guessing, cake? Only the stewards have access to the replicators."

"That's true so far as it goes," Tassa said, then rubbed her forehead with a weary sigh. "But every trip, I swear, someone figures a way around that. I'm constantly cleaning up after unauthorized parties like this one. Thank goodness this one is just some cake crumbs. The things I've had to scrub out of the carpets..." She gave up on describing it, just threw up her hands.

"Did Chou-Chou do this?" Ritchie asked.

"The Felzkinder?" Tassa said disbelievingly.

"Mr. Rose seems to think that when Chou-Chou wanted sugar, he could find ways to get it," Ritchie said. "Like breaking into empty rooms or hacking replicators."

"I don't know what Chou-Chou could get away with at home," Tassa said. "But on this train, that's quite impossible."

"How do you know for sure?" Ritchie asked.

Tassa gave Fitz a sharp look as if demanding he intervene. Ritchie *was* being a bit aggressive. But he rather thought that was a good thing.

"Can you tell for sure?" he asked, raising his eyebrows in his most pleading expression.

Tassa gave an exasperated sigh, then turned towards the door panel. She pressed her palm to it, then tapped the wall just over it. What had looked like textured wallpaper became a screen of scrolling text.

"There," Tassa said as the text stopped scrolling. "Someone opened the door a minute ago. I'm guessing that was the two of you. Then there was another opening ten minutes before that."

"Me again," Ritchie said.

"Nothing before that since the maintenance crew came through before we left the depot," Tassa said.

"But that's not possible," Ritchie said. "Look at this mess. Did your crews leave this behind from the last journey? Because the sauce smeared on that plate looks fresh."

Tassa looked down at it with a frown, then bent to pick up the plate. "You're not wrong. But the logs can't be wrong either."

"They both can't be right," Fitz said.

"Well, I'd hate to tell you what anyone else is going to think," Tassa said. "But you'd be hard pressed to convince anyone you didn't bring this plate in here yourself. All the evidence backs that up."

"Why would I do that?" Ritchie asked.

Tassa seemed to consider her words carefully. "Food-seeking behavior is a common problem stewards encounter with traveling cadets," she said at last.

Ritchie scoffed.

"Look, you know we didn't do this," Fitz said. "This morning? After everything that happened, do you really think we'd break into this room and have a cake party?"

"Well, I know *you* didn't," Tassa said to Fitz, looking at the date stamp on the log again. "You were talking to me at the time."

"Do you have any way of telling where that plate was replicated?" Fitz asked.

Tassa turned the plate over in her hands. Fitz saw no distinguishing marks anywhere on it, but he had no idea what she might be looking for.

"Come on," Tassa said, and led the way back to her alcove. Ritchie pressed close against Fitz's back to watch as Tassa put the plate into the replicator and keyed in a command.

There was a flash, and then the plate was gone.

"What happened?" Ritchie asked.

"She recycled it," Fitz said. He guessed Ritchie hadn't been kidding about her lack of familiarity with replicators. "The raw stuff is back in the system, ready for reuse."

"But—" Ritchie started to say.

"There," Tassa said, but whatever she was looking at was playing through her implant into her own visual field.

"Can't see," Fitz said.

"Oh, right," Tassa said, and did the same trick with her fingers to make an apparently ordinary section of wall become a readout screen. "There," she said, pointing to a string of numbers. Fitz just raised his eyebrows. "Right, I know you don't know the location codes. But this plate came from the kitchen."

"Can you tell what was replicated with it?" Ritchie asked.

"You mean what kind of cake?" Tassa asked.

"Sure," Fitz said.

The screen they were looking at didn't change, but Tassa's pupils were darting around, so Fitz knew she was back interfacing with her implant. "It was a pound cake," she said. "Just what the replicator had in its memory banks as your basic standard pound cake."

"With sugar," Ritchie said.

"Yeah, with sugar," Tassa said. "I can get the whole recipe if you like."

"No," Fitz said. "So no cherries?"

"Well, a cherry sauce," she said.

"Blood-cherry?" Ritchie asked.

"No, just your standard cherry," Tassa said. "Blood-cherry is too niche of an item for the replicators to have it preprogrammed."

"Hence the Lady Fabron always traveling with her own supply," Fitz said under his breath, and Ritchie nodded.

"Just the one plate," Tassa said. "No forks or anything."

"Someone was eating an entire pound cake with their hands?" Ritchie asked.

"Well, there was a knife," Tassa said. Then she frowned. "Not a standard knife."

"What do you mean?" Fitz asked. He could feel Ritchie's hand, which had been resting on his shoulder, tense up.

"Funny you should mention blood-cherries," Tassa said. Apparently, she was unaware of the dessert menu from dinner the evening before. "The replicator had been given specific instructions for a knife to be used. A Loindetu model used for cutting blood-cherry cake."

"And that's in the replicator's programming?" Ritchie asked.

"No," Tassa said. "Whoever replicated it inputted instructions to make just that knife. The replicator still doesn't know what it made, but I recognize it myself. There are a lot of Loindetu exiles here on Oymyakon, and this train line is the only public transportation. I've' noticed they tend to be traditional in their tastes. I've seen those knives before."

"One last question," Fitz said, and Ritchie behind him leaned in closer to hear the answer. "Do you know who in the kitchen replicated all this?"

"Someone on the staff," Tassa said. "They have specific permission codes per person, but there's also a general use code for when there's a rush and lots of things are getting replicated at once."

"There was a rush? Last night?" Fitz asked.

"No, but that's the code that was used," Tassa said. "Sorry. That's all I know. Now, if you'll excuse me, I have a cabin to clean up and apparently a lot of doors to double check the locks on."

11

RITCHIE AND FITZ were just stepping through the gap between cars when their path was blocked by Weld, his face nearly as red as his hair.

"Where were you?" he demanded. "You said you were going to find him and then come right back."

"I did," Ritchie said. "Look, here he is."

"What if the colonel had been looking for you?" Weld asked.

"Was he?" Fitz asked.

Weld blustered for a minute before he managed to say, "no. But he might have been."

"Well, we better get back to the cabin, then, just in case," Fitz said. "Probably better if we weren't so loud in the corridor right outside his door, too."

Weld's face darkened even further to such an alarming shade Ritchie was afraid he was about to pass out.

"Go on, Weld," she said, as he was blocking their way. "We'll be right behind you."

Weld stormed back towards the cabin.

"Don't antagonize him," Ritchie said. "Please?"

"I wasn't trying to," Fitz whispered back. "Honestly. You do realize

I'm probably going to end up with him as a bunkmate at the academy. Do you think I want to make him an enemy before we even get there? He's twice my size."

"He's only a little taller," Ritchie said.

"But quite a bit wider," Fitz added, putting his hands out to demonstrate.

"Wait a minute," Ritchie said, a sudden thought striking her. "Does that mean I'm going to end up bunking with...?"

But she couldn't say it out loud, as they were already at the cabin door. Moreau looked up as they came in, hair in mid-twirl. She didn't appear to have moved a centimeter since Ritchie had left. Her improbably blue eyes moved from Ritchie to Fitz and then across the cabin to Weld fuming in his seat.

"What's going on?" she asked.

"I found them," Weld said.

"I see that," she said.

"We were just one car over," Fitz said.

"One car over is the VIP car," Moreau pointed out. Weld threw out his hands as if to say "exactly."

"I was talking with Mr. Rose," Ritchie said. "He was all alone after suffering that devastating loss and in such a bad state."

"I see," Moreau said, still sounding bored. But the tension drained out of Weld's body and after he passed a hand over his face, his complexion was back to its normal pinkish hue.

"You were comforting him," he said. "That was kind."

"We all know how you feel about the Lady Fabron, but to Mr. Rose she was very like a mother," Ritchie said. He gave a reluctant nod, conceding at least that point. "He's all alone in the universe now, and I don't think he's quite let that sink in yet. And Chou-Chou was as much his as the lady's."

"The Lady Fabron having a heart attack after that rich cake makes perfect sense," Moreau said. "But what happened to that Felzkinder is the real tragedy."

"Yes," Weld said. He turned to look out of the window. The skies were still light, but most of the view now was of the dark, towering mountains around them. The train seemed to be picking a path through a valley so deep and so narrow it was practically a canyon.

"Were you comforting Mr. Rose as well?" Moreau asked Fitz. She finally shifted her position, putting her reader away and sitting forward so she could redo her hair.

"No, I was talking to Tassa Sokolov," he admitted.

"Do tell," Moreau said. "I saw the earring on our boy Feliks. He likes to party. I wonder if they hit the beaches of Rangeela 5 together?"

"She doesn't seem the type," Fitz said. "She actually applied to the academies every year until she was too old to keep trying. I'm not sure how she went from that to steward, but she does seem good at her job."

"So, you were interviewing her?" Moreau asked, suddenly less interested in Fitz's story.

"Kind of," he said.

"She was showing us how the replicators work and things like that," Ritchie said. Moreau raised an eyebrow at Fitz.

"I know how replicators work," Fitz said. "Ritchie meant how they work on the train. You know, how only the stewards can use them because of the security settings."

Weld scoffed without looking away from the window.

"Weld?" Ritchie asked. She told herself she wanted to draw him back into the group, but mainly when he turned his face away, she always felt like he was hiding something.

"That's right," Fitz said, as if just recalling something. "Your family worked maintenance on these trains. You know the ins and outs already."

"Not that kind of thing, surely," Ritchie said. "How much can talking about work over dinner really cover?"

"I used to play on the trains when my parents were working," Weld said. "Then later I worked on the trains myself."

"You did train maintenance?" Fitz asked.

"Just cleaning," Weld said. "But I know a thing or two about the replicators. Nothing lots of people don't already know, I'm sure."

"Like what?" Ritchie asked. He turned away from the window to look at her as if not certain if she was being sincere. He looked at Moreau and Fitz, then back to Ritchie, then seemed to decide they weren't all trapping him in some sort of elaborate practical joke. He sat forward, resting his elbows on his knees, to explain to the three of them.

"The stewards have security codes for the replicators, and the replicators keep logs to track what's created and what's recycled, right?" he said. Ritchie nodded, eager for him to keep talking. "Well, that's true as far as it goes, but there are workarounds. Mostly geared towards making the job a little less inefficient."

"Like the general code in the kitchen," Fitz said. Ritchie shot him what she hoped was a quelling look. She just wanted Weld to be comfortable talking, and Fitz tended to make Weld *not* comfortable.

"Like the general code in the kitchen," Weld said, unbothered by Fitz this once. "People tend to ask for the same things a lot. Warmer blankets, hot water, that sort of thing. There's a way to touch the panel on the replicator that sends a command to repeat the last order. It's quicker than entering in a code, and anyone can do it."

"Really?" Ritchie said.

"Tassa did say that the train lines had an issue with food-seeking cadets," Fitz said. "That must mean that at least some of them have been finding food."

"It's easy," Weld said, then reached over his head to pull down his bag. He dug through the contents and pulled out a variety of packaged items.

"What's this?" Fitz asked, picking up a foil-wrapped flat square.

"Standard issue train night pack," Weld said. "I have four in here."

"Four?" Fitz asked, then held up the pack with a "may I?" gesture. Weld shrugged and Fitz tore it open, revealing a mask to wear over the eyes and ears, a bottle of tooth-cleaning tonic, and some sort of dermal patch. "Is this a sedative?" Fitz asked, turning it over in his hand.

"Standard issue," Weld said.

"I'll take it," Moreau said and reached for it.

"You will not," Ritchie said, pushing Fitz's hand away from her. "We can't get caught with that."

"Weld just says he has four," Moreau pointed out.

"You can't be carrying that stuff around, Weld," Fitz said in his most reasonable voice.

"I wasn't going to keep it," he said.

"Well, then, why did you pack it?" Fitz asked.

"I didn't pack this stuff," Weld said, pulling something else out of his bag to thrust at Fitz. It was an enormous slab of chocolate with one corner nibbled on, the foil falling open from where it had been inadequately rewrapped. "I was hungry last night. I didn't eat any of that dinner."

"You didn't even eat the roasted meat Captain Berger gave us?" Ritchie asked. "It was pretty good."

"The colonel must have absolutely stuffed himself," Fitz said with a sympathetic groan. "I only saw him swap your cake plates."

"I wasn't going to touch any of it," Weld said with some of the old rancor back in his voice. "But later I got hungry."

"You could've just called Feliks and had him bring you anything you liked," Ritchie said.

"I looked around for him, but he wasn't out there," Weld said.

"So you went from replicator to replicator and repeated the last order?" Fitz asked, looking down at the stack of standard issue train night packs as if they finally made sense to him.

"Pretty much," Weld said. "There wasn't a lot of food, though."

"You only ate this bit of chocolate?" Ritchie asked, and Weld blushed a deep red.

"There were two slabs of chocolate," he admitted. "I'm still not hungry, and we've had no breakfast."

Ritchie felt a rush of relief that she hadn't said anything about her unfounded suspicions from the night before. He had been breaking the rules when he had sneaked out of the cabin, but only to get his hands on some food. And it couldn't even really be called stealing, since the train line provided it to all passengers. He should've called Feliks, sure, but still. It was a very minor crime, all things considered.

"Oh," Moreau said. "I guess that's why I'm hungry."

"Have some of the chocolate," Fitz said, holding it out for her, but she waved it away.

"Did any of the replicators spit out cake?" Ritchie asked. Now it was Fitz's turn to shoot her a look, but she ignored him.

"No, no cake," Weld said, snapping off another corner of the chocolate and stuffing it in his mouth before repacking his bag and rehanging it behind his seat.

"Cake sounds good," Moreau said.

"The cake came from the kitchen," Fitz said to Ritchie.

"But those berry things came from the Lady Fabron," Moreau said, not really understanding what Fitz was trying to say.

"The cake, the plate, and the knife," Ritchie said. "Why that knife, do you think?"

"Because it's terrifying?" Fitz said.

"Really?" Ritchie asked. "Because I've been thinking, and I've concluded it might be the exact opposite of that."

"What are we talking about now?" Moreau asked.

"That knife was terrifying," Fitz said to Ritchie.

"To us, but not to Chou-Chou," Ritchie said. "He sees it... well, not all the time. Mr. Rose says they don't usually have blood-cherries in cake form. But he's seen it enough not to be afraid of it. Despite the wicked sharpness and the excessive size of it and everything."

"Oh," Fitz said, then again, but longer and more drawn out. "Oh."

"What are we talking about now?" Weld asked.

"We should sneak into the kitchens," Ritchie said.

"I'm up for that," Moreau said, slapping her hands down on her knees as if about to get up.

"Sneaking?" Weld said. "No, we agreed. We'd all stay here until the colonel sent for us."

"But I'm starving," Moreau said. "And you must be too. Don't you want some real food, not just chocolate?"

"But they're not talking about finding food," Weld said, pointing at Ritchie and Fitz as if they couldn't hear everything being said. "They're talking about a knife."

"There's another knife about," Fitz told her. "A copy to the one Lady Fabron used to cut her cake. Surely you remember that knife."

"I do remember that knife," she agreed. "Oh, I see. That knife would be totally capable of slicing a Felzkinder open. And now there are two."

"We should find them both, then," Moreau said. "I suppose the other is in Lady Fabron's cabin. Unless you already found that one?"

"No," Fitz said. "We weren't in her cabin. But I really think the duplicate was the murder weapon. If we can find it and test it, maybe we can prove it."

"You can prove the knife was used to destroy the Felzkinder, maybe, but you can't prove murder," Moreau said. "Not in a strictly legal sense."

"We can't prove anything. We're just a bunch of cadets," Weld said. "Cadets who are supposed to be staying in their cabin."

Moreau waved a dismissive hand. "The colonel is not going to freak out if he finds we've gone out on our own to find lunch. Which is all it's going to look like we're doing. It'll be fine."

"Maybe Weld is right," Ritchie said and felt three pairs of eyes turn on her in wide surprise. "I mean, Fitz will always get another chance at another school. And you're only doing this to upset your mother, which you've already declared mission accomplished. But Weld and I really want this chance. And I don't know if we should risk it."

Moreau leaned back and reached for the lock of hair she was twisting before. But it was tucked back in her topknot now, so she ended with her finger extended along her temple as she regarded Ritchie with an inscrutable gaze.

Fitz took a deep breath, but before he could say whatever was on his mind, Weld was on his feet.

"Weld?" Ritchie said, but he didn't stop. He charged right out of the cabin and down the corridor towards the front of the train.

"I'd think he was going to tell on us, but the colonel is the other way," Moreau said.

"Maybe he just needs to take a walk and blow off steam," Ritchie said.

"Yes, your speaking on his behalf in such a compassionate manner clearly set him off," Fitz said. She couldn't tell if he was being sarcastic or not.

"Can we go to the kitchens, anyway?" Moreau asked. "I really have to eat something. And it is good cover for whatever the two of you are up to."

"Maybe not," Fitz said. "Ritchie isn't wrong that she and Weld have more on the line than you and I."

"Weld, who just stormed out of here?" Moreau countered.

"Fine!" Ritchie said, throwing up her hands. "Let's figure out what happened to that knife."

12

IT WAS ALMOST eerie how empty the train was. Of course, with Mr. Rose still sitting alone in his cabin, Captain Berger and the colonel were the only passengers they might run into. But still, Fitz would've expected to see more staff moving around. There wasn't even any sign of their own steward, Feliks.

They crossed the observation car and the quiet reading room car, and Fitz was just reaching towards the diner car door when it hissed open to reveal Weld facing them with his hands on his hips.

"Weld," Fitz said, drawing his hand back. "I thought you'd gone the other way."

"You wanted to check on that knife, right?" Weld said a tad aggressively.

"Among other things," Moreau said pointedly. Weld stepped back from the doorway so they could all step inside the diner. It was back in the many small booths configuration rather than the one long table they had sat at the night before, but there was no sign of anyone around. The smell of fried food lingered in the air, but only faintly. No one was cooking at the moment.

"I checked the replicator," Weld said, then waved for them to follow him to the serving counter in the far corner. Tucked away out of sight behind it was a steep, narrow staircase in the floor. Weld just barely fit down those steps, but he stopped at the bottom to wait for them to catch up.

The kitchen ran the entire length and width of the diner car, just a level underneath it. Fitz supposed the same must be true of the formal dining car, only with much more extensive kitchens. There were cooktops and deep friers and fresh ingredients in refrigerators and storage bins, all ready to be turned into real food.

There was also an entire bank of replicators set into the wall on the far side of the kitchen. Weld was already over there, tapping at a screen to show them what he had found.

"How could you even see the logs?" Ritchie asked as she reached him first. She didn't sound accusatory; she sounded impressed.

"It's easy," Weld said with a little blush. "Remember I told you how to repeat the last order? You do that like this." He pressed his fingers to hit three keys at once and the replicator lights came to full life. There was a whoosh and then a plate of steaming French fries appeared.

"Mine," Moreau said, all but lunging to take the plate out of the replicator.

"There's another plate right over there," Weld said. "It's replicating the same order as the last time I unlocked it."

"Unlocked it?" Fitz asked.

"Yeah, I was going to show you," he said, but his little glances were still all for Ritchie. "It's still on from me repeating the order, right? It thinks I'm the last person who used this again. So what I do from here is just..." He ran his fingers over more keys, then touched the wall over the pad to create a screen, much as Tassa had done. Text was scrolling, and he made it scroll faster with a flick of his fingertip until it reached the end.

"This is the log, then?" Ritchie guessed.

"Exactly," Weld said, pointing to lines of green text. "This here shows when the cake, plate, and knife were replicated last night. Or, I guess, very early this morning. But here, just an hour or so ago, someone brought just the knife back. This is the log entry for the recycling. It shows the plate was recycled separately in the VIP car."

"Tassa did that," Fitz confirmed.

"And of course, the cake was never recycled. Presumably it was consumed. The system doesn't look to get food back," he said. "But everything else is tracked. The train line doesn't like to lose replicated things; that's a loss of the raw matter. Everything is supposed to get recycled, save the food."

"Interesting," Ritchie said.

"Can you make another plate of fries?" Moreau asked, although she had only eaten a few off of the plate she already had.

"Sure, but if you want something else..." he gave the log entries another spin to set it scrolling, "I can repeat anything ordered on the logs."

"You can see what's on there?" Ritchie asked. "It looks like just numbers to me."

"It's a code," Weld said, blushing again. "It's not hard to figure out how to read it."

"How about sandwiches?" Fitz said. "Hot turkey sandwiches all around. Sound good?"

"We can bring them upstairs," Moreau said around a mouthful of fries.

"We can bring them back to the cabin," Weld said. "We really shouldn't be wandering the train."

"Have it your way," Fitz said. Weld's respect for the rules waxed and waned in a manner Fitz found deeply annoying. Total respect, total lack of respect, either one he could... well, *respect*. But this waffling was irritating.

"So we don't get to test the knife," Ritchie said with a sigh as they carried the sandwiches and plates of fries back to their cabin along with several bottles of some sort of clear, fizzy beverage unique to Oymyakon. "I wish we would've found it before it was recycled."

"No idea who recycled it, I suppose?" Fitz asked Weld.

"No, it was under the general one," Weld said. "It was done at that replicator, though, if that helps. Not the VIP one or the one in our car."

"That might help," Fitz said, but he rather doubted it. What they really needed to know was if that was what had killed the Felzkinder. All they could do now was guess.

They settled back into their cabin and set the food on the table, handing things back and forth and opening fizzing bottles and stuffing bites of hot food into their mouths. It was several minutes before any of them spoke again, but then they were very good sandwiches.

The bread was so warm, soft on the inside but with perfectly crunchy crusts that soaked up the thick, creamy gravy. The turkey was lean and juicy, if suffering a bit in comparison to the rorebeast they had eaten the night before. Still, Fitz would never have believed it all came out of a replicator if he hadn't just seen it replicated.

"How were you planning to test that knife, anyway?" Weld asked between bites. He was looking at Ritchie a touch too intensely, Fitz thought.

"Well, if we had it, we could maybe convince the train crew to do something with it," Ritchie said. "Maybe there'd even still be blood on it. Then they'd have to check, wouldn't they? At least to prove it was Felzkinder and not human."

"Or blood-cherry," Fitz said.

"Nothing has convinced them to look into anything so far," Weld said with a shrug. "I think if you had found that knife, they would still refuse to do anything, and then you'd just be more frustrated than you already are. Perhaps it's better this way."

"Perhaps," Ritchie said, but she didn't look convinced.

"What do you care one way or the other?" Fitz asked. Ritchie gave him an appalled look, which he ignored. Weld was really getting on his last nerve.

"I guess I don't," Weld said. "I'm not sorry about any of it. An evil old witch who should've been executed when the wars of acquisition ended finally got her just desserts, albeit more peacefully than I would've liked. Don't ask me to mourn for her."

"None of us do," Ritchie said. "But Chou-Chou? Surely he was innocent of anything."

"I suppose," Weld said, carefully examining a sliver of turkey from all angles before putting it in his mouth. "On the other hand, he was living a life of slavery, really. He might be glad that it's over."

"Glad?" Ritchie gasped.

"You're awfully dismissive," Fitz said.

"Shouldn't we dismiss it?" Weld countered. "It's none of our business. We're nearly at the academy, and after that, all of this will quickly become a fading memory. And what then? Chou-Chou will still be dead."

"And Mr. Rose will still be mourning," Ritchie said, setting the remains half of her sandwich back on her plate and pushing it away. "I'm not going to be so quick to forget."

"I won't either," Fitz said.

"Oh, who cares what you think," Weld said. "How long before you flunk out, anyway?"

"Not this time," Fitz said.

"Whatever," Weld said with a dismissive wave of his hand.

Fitz's vision went a pinkish-red and for a moment he was really confused until he realized that he was angry. Really, really angry.

What a strange feeling.

Weld was watching him as if waiting for him to explode. Moreau was sitting back in her seat eating fry after fry, her eyes moving from one of them to the other and back again. She was practically salivating in anticipation of a fight.

But Ritchie was just gone. Her half-eaten sandwich remained on the plate she had pushed away, but her seat was empty.

Fitz curled his hands into fists and forced himself to calm down.

Weld, hovering over him, waiting for him to make a move, made this process take a lot longer than Fitz would've thought necessary. The guy just really bugged him.

"I have nothing to prove to you," Fitz said at last, in little more than a whisper, eyes half closed and half looking down at his own fists. He willed them to loosen up and spread his fingers over his knees. They almost looked relaxed.

They weren't.

"And I have nothing to prove to you," Weld said, and turned his attention back to the last bites of his sandwich. "Or disprove."

"As you like it," Fitz said, then got to his feet.

"Wait a minute," Weld grumbled around a mouthful of hot turkey.

"No, I won't," Fitz said. "If the colonel catches me out of the cabin, so be it. I don't even care if you go find him to tattle yourself. I'm going to find Ritchie."

Only then did Weld notice that Ritchie had gone. His face went white. Then he looked confused. Fitz could practically see him playing back his memory, trying to figure out at what point she had left.

"Yeah," Moreau said, licking salt from her fingertips. "She left when you two were about to come to blows. Your bickering drove her away. Great job, everyone."

Weld looked deeply embarrassed, not meeting anyone's eyes.

But Moreau just moved over a bit in her seat to slide the remains of Ritchie's sandwich closer to her. She had only picked at any of the other food they'd been served the entire trip. She must really like those sandwiches.

Fitz left to find Ritchie.

And, he supposed, to apologize. At least this apology he could find the words for.

13

THE DOOR to the VIP car was once more locked. Fitz rather doubted that Tassa had found herself in trouble for letting non-VIPs into her car, but he wasn't surprised to see she had locked it all back down.

Even though they hadn't been the ones to leave her with extra cleaning to do. That was whoever had gotten into that other cabin. Which was still a mystery.

He ducked down into the tunnel, then emerged in the observation car. Ritchie was there, standing with her hands pressed against the glass of the observation bubble, this time looking down towards the ground.

"Looking for the knife?" Fitz asked in as close to a joking tone as he dared to try for, not knowing what she was feeling at the moment.

She looked back at him, not amused, but not angry either.

It was something.

"No," she said as she went back to gazing down between her feet. "I was watching the disks. Not looking for clues or anything. Just watching. It's kind of peaceful, how it all works."

"Oh, yeah?" Fitz said, moving closer to the bubble. She shifted to one side to make room for him to stand beside her, and they both leaned against the glass and looked down.

"No matter what's going on beneath us, and I've seen some pretty craggy surfaces down there, the disks anchor down. And once the train has passed, they just sort of launch up and sail to the front of the line and find the next anchor."

"Too bad there's not another observation car at the front," Fitz said. They could see the disks racing to the front, but they disappeared around some obstruction long before they sank down to anchor themselves in place.

"The ride is always smooth," Ritchie said. "No matter what. That raging river there, or that jagged peak we circled a minute ago back there. Always smooth."

He had a feeling she was finding a metaphor in it all. But he wasn't sure it was the best plan for both of them to get all maudlin just then.

"Ritchie," he said.

"Save it, Fitz," she said.

"Can't do it," he said and turned his head to give her an apologetic grin. "We can't give up on this."

"We've run out of clues," Ritchie said, not looking over at him, although he knew she knew he wanted her too.

"We've lost the knife," he said. "But we know it existed. That's something."

"It's not enough," Ritchie said. "People actively want to not think about this. We need a lot to change their minds, and we don't have it."

"If we can demonstrate what happened, point by point, they'll listen," Fitz said.

"But we don't know what happened, do we?" Ritchie said. "We know Chou-Chou got out of Mr. Rose's room, but how? Did he let himself out or did someone take him?"

"Has to be the first, right?" Fitz said. "Someone trying to kidnap the Felzkinder would've woken Mr. Rose."

"Unless he was lured out," Ritchie said. "Perhaps with what he loves most in the world. Sweets. Which we know were also in play. A pound cake with cherry sauce."

"A sweeter version of the thing he wanted earlier," Fitz said. "Yes, that makes perfect sense. And you were right about the knife. Using the one he was used to seeing in his lady's hand must have been deliberate. The cherry cake, the shiny knife, all so familiar. He wouldn't suspect anything."

"Not even from a stranger," Ritchie said.

"I think we're close," Fitz said. "I think we're really close."

Ritchie continued to watch the disks take off and fly to the front of the train, and Fitz watched her eyes as they tracked that movement.

Finally, he could keep silent no longer. "Ritchie?" he said.

"Fitz," she said, sounding epically tired.

"Do you really think you only get one chance? That all this is really something you could lose so easily?" he asked.

Ritchie closed her eyes with a sigh. "You know, when I was young, I didn't think so. I thought if I worked hard, I would earn things. But I've worked hard. I know I've earned the right to opportunities. But until now, I haven't been getting them."

Fitz didn't know what to say to that, so he just waited for her to go on.

She took a deep breath and then opened her eyes again. "I earned so many things I don't have. If it's that easy for me not to get them in the first place, how could I not believe they could just disappear at any moment for any reason?"

"I'm sorry I was so glib, before," Fitz said. "When I told you all about my... academic career. I'm used to seeing it a certain way. But it looks different through your eyes."

"And Weld's," Ritchie said. "I don't know his whole story, not yet, but I know he worked just as hard to get here as I did. Maybe a little harder." She finally looked over at him, just a quick glance. "I've never ruled out that even this last chance I only have because of my father's name. Just because it's closed so many doors doesn't mean this one didn't open because of him. I'll never know for sure."

"I suppose not," Fitz said. "But, Ritchie? Do you trust Weld? I mean, really trust him. Not just feel empathy for him."

"I do feel empathy for him," Ritchie said. "I'm working on the trust."

"Should trusting someone be something you work to do?" Fitz asked.

"Sometimes," Ritchie said. "Sometimes the reasons you have not to trust someone are based on bad assumptions. Prejudices or what have you. I trust my gut, you know I do, but I also like to make sure my gut isn't overreacting."

"Okay," Fitz said, turning to rest his shoulder against the glass wall of the bubble and look directly at her. "But be straight with me. Don't tell me what you wish you felt or wished were true. Tell me your gut instinct. Do you trust Weld?"

Ritchie squeezed her eyes shut, but he could see she was only shutting out the world around her so she could consult her feelings without the distraction.

"He genuinely hated the Lady Fabron," she said. "Not by association because of her family. He hated her, specifically."

"It would be educational, I think, to find some of the old propaganda she appeared in, back in the day," Fitz said. "She must have really done something with that."

"You don't know the half of it," Ritchie said. "Mr. Rose's entirely family was destroyed, probably by her husband but at least by his invading force, and on some level he must know this. And yet he adores her. Her personal charisma must have been off the charts."

"And Weld hates her," Fitz said. "If it were the Lady Fabron we'd found gutted with a knife and left to bleed out bouncing behind this train, I should be very surprised indeed if we didn't find out he was behind it."

"I think I would feel that way too, if it was just the Lady Fabron," Ritchie said. "But I'm less sure about the Felzkinder. It would be like gutting a baby and a puppy at once."

"We've seen him angry," Fitz said.

"Not that angry," Ritchie said. Then she finally turned to lean on the glass like he was doing but facing him. "We've also seen how fast he cools back down. And how quick he is to make it up."

"What, by beating us back to the kitchens to cover up the evidence?" Fitz asked.

"He didn't," Ritchie said, shocked. Then she gave it a second thought. "Did he?"

"Look, if he is the one, he's been spoofing every computer system on this train. They'll tell us whatever he wants them to tell us, and no more," Fitz said.

"Can he do that? Can cleaning up a train really teach anyone all that?" Ritchie asked.

"He's in the same boat you're in, remember?" Fitz said. "You both slipped in the last possible slot at the last possible academy. You both earned your place in a way Moreau and I didn't. I don't think underestimating what he's capable of doing is the way to go. If only we could access his school records and see what he's been studying."

He saw something light up in Ritchie's eyes. Then he saw her push it away.

"Don't do that," he said.

"Don't do what?" she asked.

"Whatever you were just thinking, you just told yourself you're wrong and you pushed it to the back of your mind," Fitz said.

"How could you know that?" she asked.

"I know you," he said. "Tell me what you were just thinking."

"No," Ritchie said with a scoff.

"Tell me."

"No," she said again and started to walk away. Then she spun on her heel to lean back towards him again, both hands on the sides of the bubble, trapping him as far back in the train as it was possible to go. "All right," she said. "Maybe I'll tell you what I was thinking, but you tell me something first."

"Okay," he said. "At my last school—"

"Not some random confession!" she said, and he stopped talking. "Tell me this. Do we really have no other suspects?"

"Well, I don't know," Fitz said. "It could be one of the many crew members, but how would we go about narrowing that down? Like everyone keeps pointing out, we're going to be at the academy soon. We only have so much time here."

"And Captain Berger?" Ritchie asked. "He had some sort of... well, not a relationship, I guess, but a feeling for the lady Fabron? And hunting skills?"

"Do you really think he'd do that to Chou-Chou and then look down his nose at the job later for our benefit?" Fitz asked. Then he found himself switching his own thinking, like flicking a switch. "Unless he did. To throw us all off his track."

"It's possible," Ritchie said. "He could have a motive. We should talk to him."

"Yeah, I bet he'd love that," Fitz said. Ritchie grinned back at him. "Okay, now tell me what you were just thinking."

At first he thought she wasn't going to, but then she pushed off the walls of the glass bubble to rock back on her heels, folding her arms as if about to give a lecture. "It was what you said before, about wishing you could see Weld's records."

"Oh, good idea," Fitz said. At her puzzled look he added, "you distract him, I take his reader? Isn't that what you were thinking? That we could hack his reader?"

"Can you hack anything?" she asked.

"I thought you could," he said. "Wait, was this not your plan?"

"No," Ritchie said with a laugh. As he just gaped at her with deepening confusion, she only laughed harder.

"Ritchie," he said warningly.

"I'm sorry," she said, and got her giggles under control. "You're overthinking it. We don't need to hack anything. We just need to ask."

She spun on her heel and started moving at double time back towards the tunnel to their car. Fitz hurried to catch up.

"Weld?" Fitz asked as he fell into step beside her.

"Not Weld," she said. "Colonel Hansen."

14

THE FIRST TIME Ritchie knocked on the colonel's door, it was with a bit of trepidation. She glanced at Fitz, who gave her an encouraging nod, and she knocked a second time with more vigor.

After her third knock went unanswered, she turned to Fitz with a shrug.

"I guess we only assumed he was in there the entire time," Fitz said. "Maybe he's on the bridge with the train commander or in one of the other public areas."

"He could be anywhere, really," Ritchie said. "Including in there, not responding."

"Hey, guys," Feliks said as he emerged from a little alcove like the one Tassa had. "Do you need something?"

"No, we just wanted to talk with the colonel, but he doesn't seem to be in," Fitz said.

"He was having lunch with Captain Berger the last I saw him," Feliks said.

"In the diner?" Ritchie asked.

"No, in the saloon," Feliks said. "I think the captain finds the diner a bit too bright. He's more of a dark wood furniture and mellow lighting kind of guy."

"We'll check there. Thanks," Fitz said.

"Do you guys need anything in the cabin?" Feliks asked. "I haven't been as attentive as I ought to have been, but I did have some extra duties because of what happened in the back of the train."

"No worries," Fitz said. "And no, we're doing just fine."

"Okay, but let me know if that changes," Feliks said, and headed out the back of the car.

"Where are you going?" Ritchie asked, as Fitz took the first step down the corridor.

"To the saloon," Fitz said.

"Maybe we should just wait for him here," Ritchie said.

"What do you mean? We're not going to step up to the bar or anything. We're just going to talk to the colonel."

"I know, but we wanted to talk to him alone, right?" Ritchie said.

"So we'll tell him that when we see him," Fitz said. Ritchie looked like she still wanted to argue, but in the end gave in with a nod and followed Fitz through the observation car, reading room, and diner to the saloon car.

Feliks wasn't wrong about the decor. He hadn't looked around much the last time he'd passed through; he had been too distracted by all the desperately drinking people to notice much else.

The change in lighting was drastic enough that the two of them stopped in the doorway to wait for their eyes to adjust. There were a few windows letting in natural light, but they were small and round like portholes, only revealing a smear of cloud and rain occasionally broken by the jagged peak of a passing mountain. The walls were covered in dark paneling that appeared to be real wood, the tables and chairs made of an even darker type of wood. The lights were meant to look like candlelight, dim and yellow and barely penetrating the shades covering them.

"Looking for someone?" a voice called out to them. It was Captain Berger. He had a loud voice pitched to carry over battlefields, which made him sound aggressive, although Fitz was pretty sure he didn't mean to be offputting. Not in that moment, anyway.

"We are," Fitz said, his sweeping gaze finally finding the captain sitting alone in the corner of the train car, his back to the wall and a massive array of food on the table before him. But the only place setting was his. "Is Colonel Hansen here?"

"He was," the captain said, reaching to a platter of sliced meat to put more on the plate in front of him. "I'm not sure where he's gone to now."

"Did he go fore or aft, sir?" Fitz asked. The captain shrugged as he spooned some sort of mashed root vegetable onto his plate next to the meat.

"I wasn't paying attention, cadet. Sorry," he said. "Are you kids hungry? I have plenty here."

"No, we just ate, but thank you," Fitz said. "Is that more rorebeast, sir?"

"This? No. This is poultry, not red meat, boy," the captain said. Fitz moved closer to his table and saw that he had indeed mistaken a rather massive drumstick for a roast.

"That must have been some bird," he said.

"It was," the captain said. "I hunted it on Ravvagge, same as the rorebeast, but it's technically not native to that world. The first few escaped from some fool's menagerie, and now the fields on the northern continent are being overrun by the damn things. Great big running things, big as horses but meaner than honey badgers. I bagged a dozen myself. I prefer rorebeast, but this isn't bad for bird meat. Try a bit."

Fitz picked up one of the smaller slices from the platter and put it in his mouth. As he was still chewing, Ritchie leaned past him to grab a piece of her own. It was dry and took a lot of chewing. The captain was watching them both with an expectant gaze.

"Flavorful," Fitz said when he at last managed to swallow the bit down.

"It would be marvelous with gravy," Ritchie said.

The captain snorted, then turned his attention back to his own food. "I prefer my meat unadorned, but to each their own, I suppose."

"Vat-grown meat really isn't the same, is it, sir?" Fitz asked. Ritchie gave him a questioning look, not sure why he was still talking to the captain when they were looking for the colonel, but she said nothing.

"Not remotely, my boy," the captain said. "But wait until you eat something you hunted and butchered yourself. That's the best sauce in the universe."

"I bet," Fitz said. "How many animals have you hunted, sir? I mean, how many kinds?"

"Hm," the captain said, as if the question stumped him. He chewed thoughtfully for a moment, then washed the meat down with a long pull from the frothy mug next to his plate. "Let me see," he said. "It must be more than fifty now. I've never kept a list. Perhaps I should look around when I get home and see if I can remember them all."

"What was the most dangerous game you've hunted?" Fitz asked.

"A rorebeast can kill you pretty easily if you don't keep your wits about you," the captain said. "But the deadliest would have to be the thorned squids of Epsilon 20. Mainly as you have to be in deep sea gear before you can get near them. But they're very smart beasts. They know just where to tap you to cut off your air supply, and with those long, venomous spiked tentacles of theirs, they can do it. You'd be dead before you even knew how close you were to one."

"And you ate one?" Ritchie asked, looking a little pale.

"I've eaten several," the captain said. "Sliced up thin and breaded and fried, they're magnificent. A shame I don't have any with me this trip or I would let you try a bit."

"But you said they were smart," Ritchie said.

"Smart, not sentient," the captain said. "There's a difference."

"You mean legally," Ritchie said.

"What do *you* mean?" he countered. Fitz caught Ritchie's elbow and gave it a squeeze before she could gather words to respond.

That wasn't where he wanted this conversation to go. It was close to it, but clearly from the wrong angle.

"I've heard of Felzkinder hunts," he said. "You don't go in for that sort of thing, do you, sir?" He strived for just the right tone, assuming such a thing was beneath the captain but willing to be only mildly surprised if the captain contradicted his assumption.

"No, not for me," the captain said, cutting another slice of meat in half before putting a forkful in his mouth. "I've been invited to a few, mind you. But no, I don't 'go in for that sort of thing,' as you say. They provide no challenge and the meat is really subpar."

"You've eaten...?" Ritchie cut her own question off with a squeak, but the captain caught her point and narrowed his eyes at her.

"That was before they were declared a sentient species," he said testily. "I don't eat illegal meat. And I don't answer to a pair of kids. Now, get on with you. Go find your colonel and leave me in peace."

"But why would anyone eat an animal designed in a lab to be kept as a pet?" Ritchie asked.

"Obviously the ones being hunted didn't look like what's his name. Chou-Chou," the captain said, his disdain from dinner the night before in full evidence now. More, now that he wasn't tempering his opinions in the presence of the Lady Fabron. "The things were meant to subsist on greens and a special nutritive drink provided by the design company. They were meant to be lean. Chou-Chou looked like he did because the Lady Fabron indulged it with whatever junk it wanted. No one would eat that thing, all fat and grease for sure. No, the ones my friend kept for hunting were fed properly. They had meat on them, sure enough. It just wasn't very good meat. And, like I said, not worth the hunt."

"We're sorry to have disturbed you," Fitz said, squeezing Ritchie's elbow before she could get the captain's dander up again.

"Eh," the captain said with a wave of his fork. He stabbed another bit of meat, but then looked up at the two of them with narrowed eyes. "Why are you asking about Felzkinder meat? Has the thing's body disappeared or something?"

"No!" Fitz said. "I mean, not that we know of."

"You can't possibly think that *I* did that to that creature?" he asked. That aggressive tone that was always in his voice was definitely tipping into outright anger now.

He certainly had seemed to hate the thing the night before. But Fitz wouldn't dare speak that thought out loud. Especially now, when a little defusing of tempers was in order.

"No," Fitz said. "Like you said, it was very badly done. Clearly not the work of a hunter."

"Well, obviously not," the captain snapped. "The creature was killed badly, and the body was thrown away. That's not hunting, my boy. Quite the opposite."

"It's murder," Ritchie said.

"Well," the captain said, backtracking. "Not legally, of course. But it is a bad bit of business."

"I wonder why they did it?" Fitz said. "Whoever it was."

The captain shrugged as he took another drink from his mug. "Who knows? The universe is full of crazies, and most of them look just as normal as you or I. I can tell you one thing, though."

"What's that, sir?" Fitz asked.

"They didn't do it for the pelt," he said, looking at Ritchie with a mischievous gleam in his eye. "There are collectors who would pay quite a lot for a Felzkinder pelt, you know, especially from such a pudgy fellow. Makes for a bigger pelt. The silver hairs would be an enhancement, not a detriment, as well. But that's not what they were after."

"How do you know?" Fitz asked. "I'm guessing you don't mean just because we found it outside the train. You're talking about something else."

"It was the cut," the captain said, his eyes still on Ritchie as he traced a line across his own chest just where the wound had stretched across Chou-Chou from armpit to hip. "Quite ruined the pelt, you see."

Fitz hustled Ritchie out of the saloon car before either she or the captain could say another word.

15

THE MINUTE they were outside the saloon car, but before they stepped back into the quiet reading car, Fitz pulled her to one side. Ritchie leaned against the window of the hatch on the side of the train, pressing her forehead to the cold glass.

"He was just trying to get a rise out of you," Fitz said.

"He succeeded," Ritchie said, closing her eyes and just focusing on the cold slowly seeping into her forehead. "Those squid things. If they could do what he said they could, how are they not also considered sentient?"

"I don't know," Fitz said. "Probably some legal thing, like they never asked. Maybe we can look into it. Honestly, I don't know how much truth there is in what he says. He sounded like he was bragging. Maybe he was exaggerating about how smart they are."

"Maybe," Ritchie said. "But maybe I'll just stick to vat meat from now on."

"Yeah, maybe me too," Fitz said.

Ritchie pushed away from the window and the two of them passed through the reading car and the observation car without seeing any sign of the colonel or anyone else. It was like being on a ghost train.

The colonel must have gone forward to the bridge car, some place they definitely couldn't go. Ritchie stopped walking when they reached their cabin, but Fitz kept going down the corridor.

"Where are you going?" Ritchie asked.

"To see if he's in," Fitz said. "He has to be some place."

"But how could he have gotten here without us passing him on the way?" Ritchie asked.

"I doubt the kitchen under the diner car and the tunnel under the VIP car are the only sub levels," Fitz said.

"Those sound like the sort of places that would be off limits to passengers," Ritchie said.

"And your point is?" Fitz asked. Ritchie threw up her hands in surrender, but followed Fitz to the end of the car.

Fitz knocked briskly. The door slid open so suddenly the colonel must have been standing just inside of it with his hand on the knob.

"Cadets?" he said.

"Can we speak with you for a minute, sir?" Fitz asked.

"Come in," he said and stepped back from the door to sit on one of the bench seats. His cabin was identical to theirs, only a mirror image being on the other side of the train. Fitz sat across the little table from the colonel and Ritchie sat down next to him.

The colonel took a small sip from a mug of dark reddish-brown tea. From the amount of steam curling up from its surface, Ritchie guessed he had just had Feliks replicate it for him.

"So," he said as he set the mug back down on the table. "Tell me, is there any part of this train you two haven't been roaming through this morning?"

"Sir?" Fitz sputtered.

"I'm just letting you know I'm aware of all you do, cadet," he said. "I'm also aware that my suggestion that the four of you stick to your cabin was just that: a suggestion and not an order."

"I'm sure you'd prefer it if we took your suggestions at full force, though, sir?" Fitz said tentatively.

The colonel just looked at him, his face as stoically impassive as ever. Ritchie scanned it over and over for any clue, but she didn't know from where she was getting the impression that he was suppressing a smile.

And yet she was sure he was.

"Just so," the colonel said and took another sip from his mug. "Now, what did you want to speak to me about?"

Fitz took a deep breath, but then sat back in his seat, looking over to Ritchie to take the lead.

She hadn't expected that, but now the colonel was looking at her too.

"Well, sir," she said. "We've been all over the train, but only because we're trying to figure out just what happened last night."

"And have you?" he asked.

"Not exactly," Ritchie said. "I mean, we don't know who did it or why."

"That does leave out a lot," he said.

"We know someone must have lured the Felzkinder out of Mr. Rose's cabin using a lure of pound cake with cherry sauce," Ritchie said. "They brought Chou-Chou to an empty cabin in the VIP car, so quietly they didn't wake the steward. They had replicated the cake, plate and knife in the kitchen using a generic security code that anyone in the kitchen can use."

The colonel blinked, but said nothing.

"The plate was left in the cabin, which was unlocked. I found it myself when I was looking for Mr. Rose. This was after the bodies were discovered. The cake had been eaten, but we know what kind it was from the replicator records."

"The knife," Fitz prompted.

"It wasn't just any knife," Ritchie said. "It was a replica of the knife the Lady Fabron had used to cut the blood-cherry cake. You remember it?"

"Indeed, I do," the colonel said.

"Whoever did it had to enter in the specs themselves, because it wasn't in the replicator's presets," Ritchie said. "We think..." she looked over at Fitz, who nodded. "We think that knife was chosen on purpose because Chou-Chou was not afraid of it. He ate all the cake and didn't panic or raise an alarm at the sight of the knife."

"There's more," Fitz said. "Whoever did it knew the train security systems very well. How to access the replicators, how to open and close doors without it showing up on the security logs. How to open an outside door and throw out the Felzkinder without any of the alarms going off."

"The train crew is looking into that," the colonel said. "Once we're all dropped off at our stops, the train will be out of commission until they know what happened in full detail. That might extend to the whole train line. It really depends on what they find and what the fix is. In short, you cadets don't need to worry about that. It's being taken care of. No one will be throwing anything off the trains while in deep space."

"That's where you were?" Ritchie guessed. "Helping them with that?"

The colonel reached for his tea but stopped with it just before his mouth. "Where I've been or am or may ever be is none of your concern."

"Yes, sir," Ritchie said. "Of course, sir."

The colonel made a small "hm" sound and took another drink of his tea, a bigger gulp now that it wasn't so hot. Then he set the mug back down. "You had some specific reason for coming to see me," he said.

"Yes, sir," Ritchie said. Her hands were starting to twist in her lap, and she forced them to lie flat, gripping her thighs. "We wondered what you knew about Weld's background."

"Cadet Cadmar Weld," the colonel said. "I know you didn't think you could just come in here and ask me to divulge confidential information without cause. To the two of you."

"No, sir," Ritchie said. This wasn't going anywhere near as well as she had hoped.

"Do you have some specific reason for wanting to know about Cadet Weld's background?" the colonel asked. His eyes burrowed into her so intently she felt like they were leaving burn marks.

"Well," she said, and glanced over at Fitz.

"I'm not asking Cadet Fitz," the colonel said, and she looked down at her own hands instead. "I might yet, but first I want to know what *you're* thinking."

"Sir," Ritchie said, her mouth suddenly gone dry. She swallowed and pressed on. "Cadet Weld left the cabin last night."

"Every cadet left that cabin after lights out last night at some point," the colonel said. "Save you."

"Yes, sir. But Cadet Weld was gone for a much longer time than the others," Ritchie said.

"What do you suppose he was up to?" the colonel asked. She remembered what he had said, about knowing where they all were all the time. Did he also already know what Weld had been up to? Was he only asking to test her?

"He told us he was looking for food," Ritchie said. "He showed us a trick. He knows where you can make a replicator duplicate its last request. It doesn't show up in the logs. He found one replicator somewhere that made chocolate bars."

The colonel gave a humorless laugh. "Nothing so unusual about that. Cadets and food they aren't supposed to have." He rolled his eyes.

"Except it means he knows how to trick replicators," Ritchie said. "Maybe he also knows how to trick doors."

"That's a sizable 'maybe,' cadet," the colonel said.

"I know, sir," Ritchie said. "That's why we wanted to ask if there was anything in his record about having skills like that."

"Skills turned to illegal ends seldom get bragged about on CVs," the colonel said. "Not when you're hoping to work in the foreign service, anyway. I can't speak to the private sector."

"We do know how he felt about the Lady Fabron," Ritchie said.

"Cadet," the colonel said in a warning tone. "Are you trying to accuse a fellow cadet of a serious crime on a mere suspicion, or do you have proof?"

"I'm not accusing," Ritchie said.

"Aren't you?" the colonel asked.

"I am," Fitz said. "I don't see how it could be anyone else but him."

"You've eliminated all the other possibilities, have you?" the colonel asked.

"Well, not *all*," Fitz admitted.

"Maybe it was an accident," Ritchie said. "Maybe the knife thing is a coincidence, and there was a struggle, and Chou-Chou was hurt. And then thrown from the train so the perpetrator wouldn't get caught."

"Is that what you think happened?" the colonel asked.

"I don't know what happened," she admitted.

"But you know Cadet Weld was involved?"

"I don't *know*."

"But you suspect?"

Ritchie's hands were twisting together again. This time, she didn't bother to stop them. She needed the distraction.

The colonel sighed loudly, then sat forward, resting his arms on his knees. "Cadet, you need to think through what you're saying to me. I ask again, are you accusing another cadet of a serious crime when you have no proof?"

"No, sir," Ritchie said miserably.

"Very well," he said. But he didn't sit back, and he didn't look away. She was still under the hot lights, as it were. "Next question. Are you willing to stake your future on his innocence?"

"What?" Ritchie asked. She understood the words, but they made no sense strung together like that.

"If Cadet Weld has done this thing, and you have a valid reason to suspect that it *was* him, not saying anything whether it was to protect him or for any other reason would also be a betrayal of all the foreign service stands for."

"Sir?" Fitz said, but the colonel's eyes never left Ritchie.

"If you have a reason to be suspicious, you have a duty to speak up," the colonel said. When she didn't respond, he leaned in even closer. "Well, Cadet Ritchie? What say you?"

Ritchie glanced over at Fitz, who looked as completely gob smacked as she felt. But he just lifted his chin, encouraging her to speak.

Whatever she said now, he would back her up. She knew that.

But what could she say?

She regretted ever coming into the colonel's cabin. But she couldn't undo that now.

"I think Fitz and I should continue investigating," she said at last. "We must continue until we either have proof of wrongdoing on Weld's part, or we clear his name."

"Very well," the colonel said, and to Ritchie's immense relief, he finally sat back in his seat. "You do realize you don't have a lot of time to accomplish this."

"Yes, sir," Ritchie said, as she and Fitz got to their feet.

The minute they were in the corridor and the door safely closed behind them, Fitz turned to hiss at her, "clear his name?"

"If he didn't do it, then we have to," Ritchie said. "He was already doomed to start at the academy not from a position of strength. We might have just made it worse for him."

"Okay, fine," Fitz said. "But come on. You don't really think he's innocent?"

"My gut says no," she admitted. "But my gut's not proof."

"So where are we going to get proof?" Fitz asked.

"I wish I knew," Ritchie said with a sigh.

16

FITZ AND RITCHIE were still standing outside the colonel's door when Moreau stuck her head out of the cadets' cabin.

"What are you two up to?" she asked.

"Nothing," Fitz said.

"I don't believe that for a minute," she scoffed. "Come on, it's indescribably boring in here. Why should I have to suffer it alone?"

"Isn't Weld in there with you?" Fitz asked. A sudden clench of panic closed around his throat, squeezing like a fist. Was he roaming the train? Was he spying on them?

"Well, sure," Moreau said. "But you know what I mean."

"I know what she means," Ritchie whispered to him. Was she teasing him? Ritchie?

"Quiet, you," he hissed back. He knew that Moreau had been a bit annoying with all of her talk of parties, but surely Ritchie didn't think that meant Moreau was into him? Because that was a ridiculous idea.

"We can't go back in there," Ritchie whispered, more serious now. "And we can't tell her why."

"I know that," Fitz said. "You do realize she'll be pissed later when she finds out we ditched her with someone we suspected of murder."

"She'll only know that—"

"If it turns out we're right," Fitz said, raising both his eyebrows until she got his point.

"Whispering now?" Moreau said and started to come out of the cabin.

"No, stay there," Fitz said, throwing up a hand in a stop gesture as if that would ever work on her. "Ritchie and I are doing a thing. For the colonel."

"A thing," Moreau repeated skeptically.

"Right," Fitz said.

"Top secret," Ritchie whispered.

"It's top secret," he said to Moreau.

"You two are terrible liars," she said, pointing first at Fitz and then at Ritchie.

But she went back inside the cabin.

"Come on," Fitz said, leading the way back towards the VIP car, then through the tunnel to the observation car.

"We've already searched this place for clues," Ritchie said.

"We can talk here, is all," Fitz said. "We need to figure out what to do next."

"What do *you* think we should do?" she asked.

"I know what I'd *like* to do," Fitz said.

"What's that?"

"Interrogate Weld," he said. "Make him confess. That would simple everything up."

"No," Ritchie said. "Can't do it."

"We could," Fitz said. "I've studied the basic techniques."

"There are rules about that sort of thing," Ritchie said. "We'd need proper equipment and a lot of legal hoop-jumping before we could even begin, or his confession would mean nothing."

"I don't mean a legal confession," Fitz said. "I'm so tired of splitting these bureaucratic hairs. You and I both know that no matter what the law says, what happened to Chou-Chou was murder, right?"

"This isn't the same hair splitting. What's the point of just making Weld tell us the truth? We might know we're right, but who's going to believe us?" Ritchie asked. "Besides, if that was all that needed to be done, the colonel could do it."

"Maybe he should," Fitz said.

"Maybe he will if we give him evidence to make him see that it's necessary," Ritchie said. "And there we are. We circled back around."

"What other options do we have?" Fitz asked. "The bots cleaned this space, no clues here. No one will do an autopsy on the Felzkinder's body, so no help there."

"We could continue to interview people, I guess," Ritchie said with a sigh. "We've talked to all the passengers, nothing left but crew. I suppose we could start with Feliks."

"There's always the possibility the murderer is a stowaway," Fitz said. "We'd have to search compartment by compartment to be sure."

"We'd need help," Ritchie said, "and permission. Not happening."

"Well, what else is there? We can't just stand here and gab at each other."

"There's the knife," Ritchie said.

"Which was recycled," Fitz said. "We saw the record."

"Did we?" she asked. "We saw *a* record, but after Tassa read us the log from the door to the unoccupied cabin, I think we know we can't trust those."

"True," Fitz agreed.

"Also, do we have any way of knowing if it was the same knife?" she asked. "Maybe the murderer recycled the original from the Lady Fabron's cabin."

"No, I doubt that came from a replicator originally. You can't recycle something not made from replicator stuff in the first place," Fitz said. "But what if there was another duplicate? They could've made one to recycle, just to make it look like it was destroyed. But why would they bring it all the way back to the kitchen to recycle it rather than use the replicator in the VIP car? And why not do the plate at the same time if they were just getting rid of evidence?"

"Okay, we have lots of questions. How do we get answers?" Ritchie asked. "Ironically, the person I most want to ask about all this is Weld."

"Seriously? You just ruled out interrogation as an option."

"No, I mean, call on his expertise. Pretend it's all hypothetical," Ritchie said.

"No, that will never work," Fitz said. "He'd be suspicious at once."

"Or he'd be innocent," Ritchie said.

"You can't ask him. Promise me you won't try," Fitz said. "I think we should just find Tassa and ask her for more help. She'll do it, I know she will."

"For you she will," Ritchie agreed.

"What's that supposed to mean?"

"She's sweet on you, as if you didn't notice," she said with a scoff.

Fitz hadn't noticed anything of the sort. He cast back in his memory for every encounter he'd had with the steward. "You're crazy," he concluded.

"Whatever," Ritchie said. "Look, you go talk to Tassa. That *is* a good place to start."

"Thanks," Fitz said. "What are you going to be doing? Besides not going anywhere near Weld? Because you promised me you wouldn't do that."

"I don't need to ask Weld," she said. "I watched what he did. I can do the same trick, replicate the last order and then get into the logs from there."

"And see what?" Fitz asked.

"I don't know, maybe nothing," she said. "But I'm going to work my way down the train and check every replicator log just to be sure."

"Why don't we do that together, then?" Fitz asked.

"Because it's tedious and maybe pointless?" Ritchie said. "But anyway, I think you'll get more cooperation out of Tassa if I'm not there. So go on. Find her and ask her for favors. If that doesn't pan out, then start checking all the replicators starting from the back of the train and we'll meet in the middle."

Fitz nodded, and Ritchie left the observation car through the tunnel.

He went to the door to the VIP car, but found it locked.

He hadn't planned for that completely foreseeable obstacle.

"Tassa?" he called, knocking on the door. He was banking on her ears being as sharp as she claimed. Otherwise, he'd keep knocking until at the very least Mr. Rose alone in his cabin got curious about the noise and let him in.

He was just raising his hand to knock again when the door slid open.

"Hey, Fitz," Tassa said, smiling up at him. A friendly but professional smile. Ritchie was clearly imagining things. "You do know I'm not technically your steward."

"I know," Fitz said. "And I'm not supposed to be in the VIP car, but I was hoping you'd bend that rule just a little bit."

"Why?" she asked.

"You accessed the kitchen logs from your replicator," he said. "Can you do the whole train?"

"Sure," she said. "What are we looking for? More cake?"

"The knife, actually," he said. "The original is in the Lady Fabron's cabin still, right?" he asked as she moved aside to let him step into the corridor.

"Actually, no," Tassa said as she shut the door and checked that it was locked before leading him back to her alcove. "I packed all of her things so they could be off loaded when we get to her stop."

"Was the knife there, did you see?" he asked.

"Yes, it was," she said. "She had a special case for it in a chest full of blood-cherry preserves. It's there now, all clean and shiny and stowed in the chest lid just where it goes."

"You saw it was clean?" Fitz asked.

"I cleaned it myself," Tassa said. "She had left it on her dining table, still sticky with blood-cherry cake."

"But not blood?" Fitz asked.

"Cadet Fitz!" Tassa cried, coming to a dead halt in the middle of the corridor. "Are you accusing the Lady Fabron of killing her own Felzkinder?"

"No!" Fitz said, putting up his hands as if to ward off a blow. "No, only that the murderer might have used the Lady's own knife and then returned it to her cabin while Ritchie and I were off chasing duplicates. It was just a theory. Not even a very good one."

Tassa's anger melted away as quickly as it had come, and she waved for him to follow her around the corner to the replicator. "There was no blood," she said. "I cleaned the blade myself. I know at first glance that blood-cherry sauce looks like blood, but having cleaned up both in my day, believe me, there's a difference."

"I believe you," Fitz said.

"Okay," Tassa said, standing with her hands on her hips in front of the replicator. She called up the display screen, then turned to Fitz. "You said duplicates. Plural. How many are we looking for?"

"Maybe it was just the one replicated in the kitchen and recycled there later," Fitz said. "This is another theory we're testing. But what if someone had replicated a knife in the kitchen, realized we were looking for it, and replicated another just to recycle it for us to see and stop looking for the first knife. The murder weapon one."

"Sounds like a complicated plan," Tassa said. "Especially for someone who didn't cover their tracks in that cabin or with the plate."

"I don't think they think they have to try very hard," Fitz said. "On account of no one official thinking this is a murder. But the knife would be different, if it had Felzkinder blood on it."

"Interesting," Tassa said, and started tapping at the replicator screen. "This is going to take a minute, and some of it I'll be doing with my implant, so if it looks like I'm just standing here, I'm not wasting your time."

"Of course not," Fitz said. But he couldn't hide his impatience to get the answers and go find Ritchie. Why had he ever agreed they should split up?

"You came alone this time," Tassa said, as if reading his mind.

"Yeah, Ritchie is checking on a different thing," he said.

"You like her?" Tassa asked.

"She's all right," he said.

"No, I mean you *like* her?" she asked again. There was something in her eyes when she stressed that word.

Crap. Ritchie was right after all. The alcove suddenly felt too narrow and confining, and way too warm.

"Well, we've known each other since we were kids," he said. "I mean, not recently, but back in the day, we were best friends."

"Then what happened?" Tassa asked.

Like he was going to start that conversation here and now, with a relative stranger. "She moved away," he said instead. Which was also true, if not remotely the whole story.

"But now you're together again, going to the same academy," she said.

"Well, you applied to the academies. You know what their policies are on relationships between cadets," Fitz said. "We're friends now, and fellow cadets."

Tassa was frowning, and at first he thought it was because of something he'd just said. But her eyes were darting back and forth as the furrow between her brows deepened and he knew she was puzzled about something she was seeing in her field of view.

"What is it?" he asked.

"It's odd," she said.

"What's odd?" he pressed. That panicked feeling was closing around his throat again. He didn't like it.

Tassa dismissed whatever she had been looking at with a hard blink, then took hold of his hand.

"We have to hurry," she said.

He wanted to demand more information than that, but the fear in her eyes was too real, too immediate. He only nodded his head, but she was already running. He raced to catch up with her, running towards the front of the train.

Where Ritchie had gone.

17

RITCHIE COULDN'T GO AFT from the saloon car, but she could tell by looking through the tiny window built into the door that the car in front of that was the bridge. She saw crew members at workstations under a dizzying array of screens and readouts and wraparound windows filled with views of mountains and spitting rain.

There was probably a replicator there for the crew's use, maybe more than one. But she was never going to get access to it.

She told herself that whoever had killed the Felzkinder would have been in the same predicament that she was, but she didn't quite believe it. She was too used to thinking of this person as capable of going anywhere and leaving no trace. Like a ghost or a ninja. Or a ghost ninja.

Could it really be Weld? It made her sad to think that it might be. What a loss his skills would be to the foreign service. But if he had killed Chou-Chou, he didn't deserve any sort of bright future.

She stepped back into the saloon car, empty of passengers. The table where Captain Berger had enjoyed his noontime feast was clean and empty now, the chairs neatly arranged for the next party of guests who chose to sit there.

She looked around and saw no sign of a replicator, but of course there wouldn't be on this level, where the passengers were. She crossed the room to the bar and looked over the counter. Another staircase, this one with a hatch closed over it, probably to keep the bright light from the kitchens from marring the cozy darkness of the saloon.

At first, she thought the hatch was locked, but it was just catching on the latching mechanism and a good tug freed it. She saw nothing below but darkness and had to remind herself there was nothing frightening about a room with no one in it being dark. She climbed down the stairs, shutting the hatch gently behind her.

The room's sensors detected her before she was even all the way down the steps, and the lights flickered on with the same over-brightness as the ones in the kitchen under the diner. The space was much the same, if more dominated by containers of wine, beer and spirits than with food.

But the back wall was still all replicators.

Despite what she had said to Fitz, she wasn't absolutely sure she remembered what Weld had done. But she arranged her fingers in what she thought was the right configuration on the keys and pressed them down all at once.

The replicator whirred to life and created a thick slab of chocolate wrapped in shiny, untouched foil.

So this was how far aft Weld had gone in his midnight hunt for snacks. She recycled it, then brought up the logs, but she didn't understand what she was looking at. She read through the numbers, anyway. If she did this at every replicator, sooner or later she'd start noticing patterns.

Like Weld said, it was a code. She could learn how to read it.

She stepped over to the next replicator and gave it the same repeat command. This time she got a mug of reddish-brown tea just like what she had seen the colonel drinking. He must have had one here when he was lunching with the captain. Or he had ordered one made to bring back to his cabin just before they'd gone to see him.

Curious, she took a sip. It was almost too hot to drink, and her first impression was mainly of near-scalding pain. Then the flavor hit her: smoky and sweet. But the smoky taste wasn't like with the uber coffee bomb back at the depot. That had more of a roasted note to it. This was more like someone had burned tea leaves to ash and only then used them to make beverages. Not good.

And the sweetness was overwhelming, even for her tastes. How did the colonel drink this stuff?

She set it back in the replicator and recycled it, then checked the logs.

The first row of numbers was the same all the way down, and the same as on the first replicator. That must tell which car, and the second row specified the replicator. So that was something figured out. But there were dozens more strings of numbers that still meant nothing to her.

The third replicator provided her with a pound cake in cherry sauce on a white plate. And next to it: a Loindetu serving knife.

Okay, now she was getting somewhere. She set the cake and knife on the table behind her, then pulled a work stool closer to the replicator.

Now she could try to figure out which part of the code said, "knife not in my presets". She sucked a bit of cherry sauce off her thumb as she scrolled.

She couldn't tell which numbers meant "knife not in my presets," but she was pretty sure she could read the time stamp. The same order of plate, cake and knife had been placed late the night before. Before the bodies were found.

Wait, had they come from here and not the diner kitchen? Was she reading things wrong?

No, the location stamping, she understood. So she and Fitz were right about the duplicates floating around. Was the knife from here the one that had done the murder, or the one recycled in the diner, or both?

She looked at the numbers again. Those three items had been replicated the night before, and again just now, when she had done it.

But between the two was another entry, from just minutes before.

What did *that* mean?

A prickle ran up the back of her neck. She was afraid she knew exactly what it meant.

It meant that Fitz was right. She shouldn't have done this alone. She had to get back to Fitz. Now.

Ritchie jumped up from her stool, every muscle in her body tensed in preparation of a run, but she never made it more than a step before hitting a wall that hadn't been there a moment before.

She fell back, sprawling on the floor, sliding on her butt until she slammed into the corner. She shook her head to clear it, then looked up.

"Weld," she said, rubbing at the back of her head where it had impacted with the wall behind her. He wasn't standing over her or doing anything threatening. It was almost like he didn't even realize she was there as he stepped up to the replicator she had just been working at and started pressing keys.

Except he *did* realize she was there. He hadn't knocked her down, her trying to break into a run and colliding with him had done that. But he hadn't extended a hand to help her up, either.

There was no seething rage or declarations of innocence or anything at all. There was just Weld touching a replicator.

She didn't think he was there to help with the investigation, but pretending like she thought he was might be the better play. The last thing she wanted him to feel was threatened, she knew that for sure.

"Hey, Weld," she said, getting to her knees with a little help from the wall behind her. "I didn't see you. Say, I've been trying out your trick. I made one of those big slabs of chocolate with that replicator there. Pretty cool."

He looked at her, his face a frightening blank. Like all of his emotions were muted out. Like he was dead inside. Then he turned to look at the cake and knife on the counter next to the replicator. Great. How was she going to explain that away?

"I also made that," she said. "I guess that's a more common order than we thought. Sort of blows holes in all our theories. You were right. There's no point in digging into any of this. We'll be at the academy soon. Right?"

"I really wish you had stayed out of it," Weld said as he picked up the knife. The shining blade reflected the kitchen lights with a blinding flash. "I really wish you had."

He sounded exhausted. And deeply sorrowful. It was triggering an innate impulse in her, that outward grief. She wanted to throw her arms around him and lend him some comfort and strength, to buck him back up.

But she didn't like the way he was turning that knife about, watching the light reflect down one side of the blade and then up the other, over and over again. It was hypnotic.

"Are you going to stop me if I try to leave?" Ritchie asked, dropping the pretense of friendly cheeriness.

"I have to," he said. "I can't lose this opportunity."

Was he serious? "Don't you see you already have?" Ritchie asked.

"I can fix what you found," Weld said, glancing over at the replicator. "And I'm really sorry, but I can fix you, too."

"Fitz knows," Ritchie said. "Fitz knows everything I know."

"Fitz suspects," Weld corrected her. "You didn't know for sure until just now. He doesn't know anything."

"Are you going to fix him, too?"

"If I have to," Weld said, again with that sad tone. Like he was being smothered in regret, but for things he hadn't quite done yet.

"You don't have to do this," Ritchie said. She put every bit of sincere pleading from one struggling cadet to another in her voice, but he never even looked up at her. Which made it easier for her to step forward and grab the stool she had been sitting on a moment before.

She swung it with all her might. She had never swung a stool before in her life, but she had participated in every program of fight training her satellite space station had offered. Her body knew how to maximize the velocity of that stool in the tight space she had available to swing it.

And she didn't hold back. She aimed it right for his head.

The end of one chrome leg caught him just behind the ear and he went down like someone had just turned the gravity simulator up to maximum.

She watched him for a moment, stool poised over her shoulder, ready for a second swing, but Weld didn't stir.

She had to go. She had to find Fitz and the colonel.

She flung the stool at Weld's fallen body, then ran for the stairs. Weld had left the hatch open; that saved her a second's time. Then she was up in the dim light of the saloon.

She ran down the center of the room to the door towards the back of the train, but it didn't open at her touch. She hit it again and again, found the control panel and hit that, but the door refused to budge.

She heard a clatter from below. The stool hitting the floor.

Ritchie spun and ran towards the front of the train, but that door too refused any of her attempts to budge it. She yelled as loudly as she could towards the bridge car, but no one responded.

"There's another door," Weld said from behind the counter. He had made it up the stairs, but Ritchie wasn't sure how. A thin trickle of blood was coming out of his ear and he looked as gray as a corpse.

"What door?" Ritchie asked, moving to put tables between him and her. The tables might be too heavy for her to throw, but there were also plenty of chairs.

She just had to play for time. Fitz would come looking for her. She only had to keep Weld talking.

"That one," Weld said, pointing to the wall opposite the bar. As if on his magical command, a section of the dark wood paneling retreated. A square hatch, the edges becoming brighter lines of light that expanded as the hatch swung open.

And the saloon car was filled with wind and freezing rain.

"Go ahead," Weld said, still in that deadpan voice. "Try your emergency comm. Try doing anything at all with your implant. You can't, can you?"

"How did you do that?" she asked, realizing it was true. Her implant wouldn't even tell her what time it was.

But he just shook his head. "I was so hoping it wouldn't come to this. I really liked you, Ritchie. We could've been a team, you and I. Us against them at the academy. We could've topped them all. But you had to choose Fitz instead. Fitz!"

"What are you talking about?" Ritchie asked. "This isn't about the academy. This is about what happened here on this train."

"I'm sorry about that too," he said. "I get angry sometimes. I know that. But I can calm myself down too. When I want to."

"But you didn't want to," Ritchie said.

"No," he admitted. "Not last night."

"You killed the Felzkinder," Ritchie said. "To get to the Lady Fabron."

"I didn't intend for her to die," he said, but there was no regret in that statement.

"No, you wanted her to live," Ritchie said. "You wanted to destroy the very last thing she loved and then force her to go on living with the grief."

"Can you blame me?" he asked, raising his hands.

His pallor was looking pinker, not so gray and corpse-like. Ritchie didn't think that was a good sign. Not for her, anyway.

"You'll find my body harder to hide than a Felzkinder's," she said. "Not that you did such a hot job of that."

"I didn't know he was going to be pulled along with the train," Weld said. "But I've studied up on it now. I know how hard I'll have to hit you to knock you far enough out the door that the train's anti-gravity disks won't grab you. You'll land on some rocky slope or in some white-water river, and no one will ever see you again."

"And the train's security systems won't record a thing," Ritchie guessed.

Weld gave a humorless laugh, then finally started walking towards her, winding his way through the tables and chairs. "No one besides the two of us even knows that door's open right now."

"But there's one more thing you should know, Weld," Ritchie said, gripping the back of the chair in front of her, ready to pick it up the moment he got just a little closer.

"What's that?" he asked.

"You'll find that I'm also harder to kill than a Felzkinder," she said.

"Maybe," Weld said, raising the knife so that the grayish light from the world outside could flash along the length of the blade. It wasn't blinding like the kitchen light, but it made its point.

She remembered what the colonel had said about that shallow cut and how long it had taken Chou-Chou to die. If Weld cut her the same way, she'd still be alive for a long time afterwards. Only she wouldn't be bouncing along behind the train waiting for rescue.

No, she'd be alive but plummeting down through the storm, out of the range of the antigravity disks, watching the mountainside below rush up to meet her.

18

RITCHIE WASN'T ANSWERING his calls. Worse, his implant was quite firm in its belief that she wasn't even on the train.

He had a momentary surge of panic that abated a bit when further questioning his implant revealed that, as far as the train was concerned, Ritchie had never boarded at all.

He knew that wasn't true. It opened the possibility that the systems were wrong about everything else. Maybe she was still okay.

The observation car, the reading room car, and the diner were all empty. He raced through them with only the briefest of glances around and a quick call of her name that never got any response.

Even if she were in the lower levels where the replicators were, she should hear him. He was certainly being loud enough.

Then he reached the saloon door, colliding with it when it failed to open at his approach.

"What's going on?" he demanded, pounding at the door and then punching any button at all on the control panel.

"It's sealed," Tassa said, waving him away from the control panel so she could try entering things with a bit less violence. Fitz looked out of the hatch on the side of the airlock at a scurry of gray clouds parting around a jagged mountain peak, like the rocks were a knife edge slicing through the cottony fog. Then he pressed his face to the saloon door glass.

"Ritchie!" he called. He was starting to get a little hoarse.

"Even if she's in there, she can't hear you," Tassa said. "The door is too thick."

"But she's in there, right? You know she's in there? That's why we ran this whole way?" Fitz said.

"Why were we running?" Feliks asked. Fitz hadn't even noticed the steward was there, but there he was, as winded as Fitz and Tassa were.

"When did we pick *you* up?" Fitz asked.

"I saw you run by, and Tassa was sending out a code red," Feliks said. "What's going on?"

"The door is sealed," Tassa said grimly. "It shouldn't be. And no one from security is answering my pages."

"How is that possible?" Feliks asked.

"Tassa, what did you see?" Fitz demanded.

"The knives," Tassa said, sitting back on her heels. She was still touching the control panel but had run out of things to try for the moment, apparently. "Someone was replicating more of them here."

"How many?" Fitz asked.

"Three that I saw," Tassa said. "I found it a little alarming."

"We have to get in there," Fitz said, cupping his hands around his eyes to try to see inside. "It's all fog; I can't see a thing. I'd swear it's raining in there."

"Someone locked the door to hide the knives?" Feliks asked, confused.

"Ritchie is in there with whoever killed the Felzkinder," Tassa whispered to him, but the airlock magnified her words perfectly clearly.

"With Weld," Fitz said. "I see his head."

"My implant says Weld isn't on the train," Feliks said. "Wait, it says—"

"That he was never on the train," Fitz said. "Yeah, catch up."

"Okay, I can access some of the system in the saloon car," Tassa said, her eyes all but rolled back in her head. "Two heat signatures. One has to be Weld, from the size of it."

"Is the other Ritchie? Is she okay?"

"I can't really tell," Tassa said. "What's going on in there? Are the climate control systems way out of whack?"

"There's a door," Feliks said. "It's disguised in the paneling and no one uses it since there's another at the kitchen level, but there *is* a hatch on the side of the car at that level."

"Wind and rain," Fitz said. "That's what I'm seeing."

"The system won't let me close it," Tassa said, but there was a grimly determined set to her mouth.

"If anyone outside of security can do it, Tassa can," Feliks said to Fitz. "She just needs time."

"Ritchie might not have time," Fitz hissed back. He turned to punch at the door again, but all he was doing was bruising his hand.

"Cadet!" the colonel said as he appeared at the far end of the diner and double-timed to the saloon door. "Calm yourself at once."

"Ritchie is in there!" Fitz said. "With Weld! He's going to kill her."

"He's not going to kill her," the colonel said.

"He knows we're on to him, sir!" Fitz said.

"Doubtless," the colonel said, moving Fitz to one side to examine the door himself.

"He's got nothing to lose now," Fitz said.

"I've heard you, cadet," the colonel said. "I didn't say Weld wouldn't attempt to harm Cadet Ritchie. I only said he would not succeed."

"You have someone on the other side of this door?" Fitz asked, trying to peer through the window again.

"I do," the colonel said. "Cadet Ritchie."

"Weld is twice her size," Fitz said.

"And he's trained half as hard," the colonel said. "Cadet Ritchie can handle herself just fine."

"Sir," Fitz said, forcing himself to take a breath and get some of the shrillness out of his voice. "With all due respect. Ritchie will fight fair. We already know Weld will not."

The colonel's inscrutable black eyes locked with his, like he was seeing Fitz for the first time. Like he hadn't been worth the colonel paying attention to until this moment.

"Sir, Ritchie feels sorry for him," Fitz said. "Even now, when he's clearly insane, she will still do everything she can to see that no harm comes to him."

"She won't spare him," the colonel said. "She knows what is expected of a guardian. If it comes down to his life or hers—"

"She won't choose his life over hers, but she will hesitate," Fitz said. He instantly regretted interrupting the colonel and braced himself for a dressing down that he was actually going to feel for once.

But it never came.

"You might be right," the colonel said, and looked down at Tassa, still sitting with her face close to the control panel. "Is there any hope of opening this?" he asked her.

"I'm working," she said, speaking vaguely as if her mind was far away. "I can't say."

"There are more replicators under the diner," Feliks said. "Nothing in the presets is really going to help, though. Do you have specs for any kind of cutting instrument that I can feed to a replicator? Something to get through this hatch?"

"That would be a complex build. It would take some time," the colonel replied.

But Fitz was looking at the outside door set in the side of the airlock. He reached for the locking mechanism and found that it turned easily under his hand.

"Cadet," the colonel said warningly.

"Replicate rope," Fitz said to Feliks. "It's quick and in the presets, right? Just make me some rope." He looked over at the colonel. "Otherwise I'm going out without it. Hope that the train's antigravity disks catch me."

Feliks looked from the colonel to Fitz, then back again.

"Well, you heard the cadet," the colonel told him. "Get him some rope, ASAP."

"Sir," Feliks said, and sprinted into the diner, launching over the counter to slide down the stair railings to the kitchen below.

"You have any training with this, cadet?" the colonel asked.

"With climbing on the outside of moving trains? No," Fitz said, but mustered a grin. "How hard can it be? And you're going to be coming in that door in a minute or two anyway, right?"

"Yes, we are," the colonel said, looking down at Tassa. "I like this girl. We could use more cadets with her drive to solve problems."

"You could've had her," Fitz said. "She applied every year she qualified, but never made the cut."

The colonel's mouth drew into a tighter line, but whatever he was thinking, he kept to himself.

"Rope," Feliks managed to get out between gasps for breath and thrust a long coil of it into Fitz's hands. It was still warm from the replicator.

"There's a ring in the back of your uniform belt," the colonel said, turning him around by the shoulders, then digging at the belt at a point in the small of Fitz's back. Fitz felt something pull free from the belt itself, then the rope was sliding through it, the rope whistling through the metal ring as the colonel pulled it through in a smooth motion.

"There's a latch just outside the door," Feliks said. "I replicated hooks as well."

"Let me tie it," the colonel said, and Fitz tried to see what was going on behind him. "You're going to be tethered to the train," the colonel explained as his hands raced through a series of intricate motions. He was using a very specific knot to tie the rope to the hook, clearly something he knew well.

Just what was the colonel's story?

"If you fall off the train, the antigravity disks will catch you," Feliks told him, but before Fitz could feel too much relief he added, "of course they might just shove you straight back up and pulverize you against the bottom of the train. So try not to fall off."

"Great, thanks," Fitz said.

"Also, if you move away from the train with enough velocity, you'll be outside of the range of the antigravity disks. Then you'll just fall," Feliks said.

"How would I be moving away from the train with velocity?" Fitz asked, trying to picture it.

"If you jumped away from it," Feliks said.

"Or were pushed," the colonel said, turning Fitz by the shoulders again, this time to face the hatch.

"Ritchie," Fitz said, imaging Weld throwing her out of the train.

"Exactly," the colonel said. "Get going. We'll be with you momentarily."

"Yes, sir," Fitz said.

Then the colonel spun the hatch open and swung it out into the wind. Fitz put an arm across his face as needle-like jets of freezing rain pelted him.

What was he thinking?

He was thinking that Ritchie needed him. And he wasn't going to let her down. Not this time.

The colonel was yelling something, but it was lost to the storm. Then he grabbed Fitz's hand and pressed something into it.

Goggles.

Fitz put the goggles over his eyes and looked around.

Most of the world around him wasn't that much clearer, but he didn't need to see far. Just far enough to pick the next handhold. Then the next.

He grabbed a metal rung outside the hatch and swung out into the wind. Then he was slamming against the side of the train, hard enough to knock all the air out of his lungs.

He just clung there for what felt like an eternity, fighting to get his breath back, to lift his head against that wind and to peer forward along the side of the speeding train.

He could see the open hatch in the side of the saloon car. It wasn't far. It was only a few meters. Into the wind, but still.

Only a few meters.

He started to crawl.

19

RITCHIE MANAGED to swallow down her fear of that knife, throwing over the three tables closest to her to make a sort of barricade around the corner she was standing in. Then she dropped into a fighting stance and waited for him to draw closer.

Then he pulled out another knife he had been keeping tucked away at the back of his belt.

Those Loindetu cake knives were really short swords.

Some of what she was feeling must have shown on her face, because Weld lowered the blades he was holding crossed in front of him and said, "I don't have to cut you."

"That's what I've been telling you," Ritchie said.

"No, I mean, I don't have to cut you first," he said. "One way or another, you're going out that door. You're going to hit the side of that mountain. Depending on how far below it is beneath us at that given moment, you might hit terminal velocity first or you might not. But you're going to end up smashed on the ground. But if the knives scare you, I don't have to cut you first."

"I'm not jumping out on my own," Ritchie said. "Come on. You don't really think I'd do that?"

Weld just shrugged. "It's not going to change how this all ends. You can't win."

"If I believed that every time I heard it, I wouldn't be here now, in this uniform," Ritchie said. She was getting angry now. A little bit of that was something she could use in a fight, but too much would make her sloppy. "Do what you're going to do."

He shrugged again, as if he didn't really care how things went down.

Then he lunged, dropping into a low, extended thrust with one of the blades raised over his head and the other jabbing at her from between two of her table barricades.

So. He had done some fencing.

So had she.

Ritchie avoided the stab easily enough, spinning to grab one of the fallen tablecloths that lay in a bunch on the ground. She flung it straight in his face. It unfurled as it flew through the air like a fisherman's net. He fell back as he clawed at the cloth that was now covering his eyes.

She had hoped in that scuffle he would drop one of the knives, but no such luck. She picked up a chair and threw it at him. He knocked it aside, but with a bellow of rage.

Good. That calm demeanor had really been freaking her out. Anger at least had a normalcy to it.

She threw the only other chair that was behind her barricade. He ducked his head and took the impact on his shoulder with a grunt, but then he kept coming.

Ritchie waited for him to get closer, then kicked one of the barricade tables at him. It shrieked as it slid across the floor. He dodged around it, moving with a lumbering slowness that would've been comical to watch in other circumstances, but in this one proved just adequate to the moment. He tripped over one of the legs but was otherwise unharmed.

Then, with a burst of speed she hadn't been expecting, he swung out at Ritchie. She fell back against the wall but couldn't get far enough away to avoid the blade that sliced across her forearm, cutting away the sleeve of her uniform tunic but only just grazing her skin.

"Shallow cuts," Weld said as he fell back just a step. Not pressing his advantage. Taunting her. He thought he had all the time in the world to get to her.

Ritchie yanked off the torn tunic, then dropped back into her fighting stance.

"Showing off?" Weld sneered. Ritchie didn't react. She knew what he was thinking. With the tunic on, she looked like any other cadet, but with just the tank top beneath, every muscle she had fought so hard to earn stood out in stark relief.

She had trained. Hard. And it showed. But not when she was in uniform.

But showing off her muscles wasn't why she had taken the tunic off. She lifted a hand and made a quick come-get-me gesture with her fingers.

Weld scoffed again, then lunged at her. He might have studied some fencing, but he hadn't studied it well. He repeated the same motions that we're far from refined. She knew exactly where his blade was going to go.

She snapped her tunic out to its full length, then wrapped it around the knife's blade, pulling it back with a jerk Weld wasn't prepared for. It flew out of his grasp, whistling through the air to sail out the open door, out into the storm. She imagined it torpedoing down to the embed itself in the rocky landscape below.

One down. One to go.

Weld was shaking his injured hand and looking towards the open door like he wasn't sure what had just happened or where his knife had gone. But he recovered quickly, emitting another bear-like bellow of rage.

Ritchie had a split-second to wonder whether he controlled his anger the same way he implied he controlled his cooling off, if he was working himself up into a state of red-hot rage just for her benefit. Then he was charging at her, flinging a table out of the way with his now free hand and swinging at her with the other blade.

It was his left-handed blade, not his dominant hand. His swing was clumsy and a little slow.

But freezing rain had been blowing in that open hatch for several minutes now. The parquet floor was slick with water that was in the process of becoming a sheet of ice. The vault that should have taken her cleanly over the remaining table instead had her tumbling over it as the foot she was launching off of slipped out from beneath her.

She got over it, though, rolling away from Weld's reach and fleeing to the opposite side of the car.

He turned to her, and she saw a trickle of blood running down the blade in his hand, quickly washed away by the rain.

Then she felt a line of fire across her shoulder blades. He had cut her. Somewhere in there, he had gotten a lucky strike in.

She didn't think he had cut her too deeply, given the small amount of blood on the blade. But when he advanced toward her and she tried to move her feet into her fighting stance, she found herself lightheadedly dropping to one knee.

Not good.

Her vision was getting a little dark around the edges as well. But she knew Weld was advancing on her. She could hear his footsteps, his labored breathing.

She almost felt like she could feel the way his mass was parting the rain that blew all around them.

She pushed herself back up to her feet, ignoring the defects in her vision, and focused on that other sense of where he was in space.

His hand clutching the remaining knife. He was going to do that same lunge again. Where would that hand be?

His breath changed just before he started to lunge, and Ritchie fell back, but only to shift her balance to her back leg. Her front leg executed a somewhat imperfect circle kick, but it was enough to send the second knife out the open hatchway.

Then she was on her hands and knees on the freezing, wet floor. She was going to pass out in about a second. She didn't know how to fight that.

All Weld had to do was wait a moment. Then he could throw her inert body from the train, and there was not a single thing she could do to stop him.

But waiting wasn't something Weld was prepared to do. Not in that moment. The sense she had had before, that he was summoning rage, was all gone now. No, the rage was definitely controlling him. She lifted her head to look up at him, just able to make out his face through the blowing rain and the darkening of her vision, and saw nothing but murderous rage in his eyes.

His hand caught a fistful of her hair and yanked her painfully to her feet. He dragged her towards the hatchway, her feet skittering uselessly over the icy parquet flooring. But he didn't bring her to the very edge. Instead, he flung her towards the hatchway from far enough away that she was able to twist and catch hold of the very edge of the hatch.

For all the good that did her. She clutched at the handle that circled the outside of the hatch, but her legs were blowing in the wind from the train's motion, dragging her body away from the opening.

Even if she weren't about to pass out, she'd only be able to hold on in those circumstances for a minute, maybe two.

But she was about to pass out. And the way her whole body hurt, she found a part of herself welcomed the thought.

But she shoved that part way to the back of her mind, focusing on her fingers curling over the icy handle, and forced them to hold on. Just hold on.

The wind around her was dragging her back from the hatch, but it was also buoying her up. It almost felt like an arm wrapped around her, keeping her from falling.

"Ritchie!"

Ritchie willed her eyes to open, but she still didn't believe what she was seeing. "Fitz?"

That *was* an arm wrapped around her. And it was not just holding her up, it was pulling her back to the open hatch.

"Weld!" she cried.

"Hold on!" Fitz told her. He had pulled her close enough so that she could wrap an arm around the handle outside the hatch door, a surer grip then her fingertips. But Weld's head was poking out into the storm, looking for her. Ritchie called out in alarm, but Fitz already saw it.

He took the sparest of moments to be sure she was holding on tight.

Then he let her go, jumping to catch at the handle over the hatch door then swinging inside, kicking Weld in the chest with both feet at once.

Weld fell back into the saloon, out of Ritchie's sight. But any elation she might be feeling was dim and far away.

Her arm was slipping.

She closed her eyes and hugged the handle tighter, but the pull of the wind was too strong. The pelting rain on her face was like a steady barrage of needles. And she was so very tired.

"Ritchie!" Fitz called again. "Let go! I have you! Let go!"

She wanted to open her eyes and see what was going on, but her eyelids were frozen shut. She had to take him at his word.

She let go. There was a dizzying rush as she tumbled, out away from the train. Then there was a snap, like she'd reached the end of a tether.

And then she was pulled back in. Back inside the freezing wetness of the saloon interior, but at least she was out of the wind.

She felt a warmth on her face. Fitz's hand, melting the ice on her eyelashes.

"To be honest, I wasn't sure that was going to work," he said.

"Weld!" Ritchie said, grasping at Fitz's arm in alarm. She still couldn't open her eyes, but she didn't feel Weld near. Where had he gone?

"It's all right," Fitz said. "He's out of it in the corner over there."

"Over where?" Ritchie asked, pushing his hand away from her face and forcing her eyes to open.

"Just there," Fitz said, pointing to a now-empty corner. "Wait a minute. Where did he go?"

Then Weld was back, charging up the stairs from the kitchen, two more knives in his hand.

It was all about to start all over again.

But then the door to the diner car just exploded. Fitz's arms tightened around her as he protected her head. But the door wasn't coming their way.

It was blasting across the length of the car, just where Weld was standing at the top of the stairs. He tried to spin out of the way, but the molten edge of the door caught him and sent him tumbling back behind the counter.

"That did it," the colonel said as he stepped into the sodden saloon with some sort of large-bore gun in his arms. He looked back over his shoulder at Captain Berger. "You're right. This thing can punch through a reinforced hatch."

"Rorebeast hide is thicker than an armored tank," the captain said.

"I'm dreaming," Ritchie murmured.

"You're not," Fitz said.

"Okay, but I *am* going to pass out now," she said.

"Go ahead, cadet," Fitz said. "You earned it."

20

THE COLONEL PUT Weld in restraints, then escorted him back down the train to his own cabin, refusing the offers of help from the train crew.

It was an Oymyakon Foreign Service Academy matter.

Fitz followed along behind, fuming. Yes, it was an academy matter, but only because the only part the other authorities cared about was the damage to property. Again.

But at least Weld was facing some consequences.

The colonel put Weld in his own cabin but left his door open as if inviting Fitz to listen in from the corridor. He leaned against the wall, just out of sight from the doorway.

"Cadmar Weld," the colonel said, and Fitz heard a little hiss of breath as Weld realized he was no longer being addressed as a cadet. "Do you have anything you want to say?"

"Is this an official record?" Weld asked.

"It can be, if you like," the colonel said. "I'm going to order some tea. Would you like anything?"

"Will you take the restraints off?"

"I don't think so, no."

"Then no," Weld said bitterly.

The colonel poked his head out into the corridor and saw only Fitz there, leaning against the wall with his arms crossed and a dark glower on his face.

"Where's our steward?" the colonel asked.

"I think he's still helping Tassa with Ritchie," Fitz said.

"Ah, yes," the colonel said. "In the VIP car. Of course. Well, can you do that little trick all you cadets know to make me a mug of my tea?"

"Yes, sir," Fitz said, although there was little in the world he wanted to do less.

"Thank you, cadet," the colonel said. He started to go back into the cabin and turned back to Fitz again instead. "Cadet, when the train doctor has finished with Ritchie, have him give me a report. Tackle him in the corridor if you have to."

"Yes, sir," Fitz said. That he would more gladly do. He was irritated enough they had refused to let him help move Ritchie to one of the VIP cabins or even stay with her.

He went into Feliks' alcove and looked at the replicator, then arranged his fingers on the keys in the correct pattern. He was expecting to have to go into the logs to find the last time the colonel had ordered tea, but it turned out to be what was replicated when he duped the last order. He picked it up and carried it back down the corridor and knocked briefly on the colonel's doorframe before carrying the mug inside.

"Ah, thank you, cadet," the colonel said, reaching out to take the mug from Fitz's hands.

Weld didn't look up at Fitz, to Fitz's disappointment. He had been hoping for at least that much closure between them. But the colonel cleared his throat and Fitz knew he had to leave the cabin without letting Weld know just how much he hated him.

Fitz went to resume his position outside the door, only to find Moreau already standing there.

"What are you doing out here?" she asked.

"Listening in," Fitz hissed at her. "Now hush."

"Listening to what?" she asked, trying to lean around him to see into the room. Fitz grabbed her arm and propelled her back down the corridor towards their cabin, but stopped without going inside it.

"Weld's in there," Fitz said. "He's about to confess everything."

"Is he?" Moreau asked with interest.

"He is, or I'll beat it out of him," Fitz said.

"Where's Ritchie?" Moreau asked.

"Don't you know?" Fitz asked.

"How would I know anything? No one tells me a thing," she said. "You and she went out on your top-secret mission. Then Weld left and refused to say why. So it was just me, sitting alone in the cabin, bored out of my mind. Wondering why I'm the only one who's following the rules. Wondering when I became the person that even cares about the rules."

"Oh, stop it," Fitz said, annoyed. "You act like this is all a lark to you, but I don't believe it. You want to be here. And it's not just about your mom."

"You know me so well?" she asked.

"No, and that's on me," Fitz said. "But if there's one thing I learned on this trip, it's to pay attention to the people around me."

"Well, I'm honored," Moreau said. "But seriously, where's Ritchie?"

"Fitz!" Tassa called out from the end of the corridor.

"I'll catch you up," Fitz promised, then left Moreau's side to go to Tassa. "How is she?"

"Awake now. The doctor says she'll be fine," Tassa told him.

"Thank goodness. When she blacked out like that..." he ended in a shudder.

"There was a toxin on the blades that cut her," Tassa told him. "It wasn't part of what was replicated with the knives."

"Then how did he get it?" Fitz asked.

Tassa looked around as if to be sure they weren't overheard, then leaned in to speak close to his ear. "He stole it from Captain Berger. It was in with his hunting supplies. The captain didn't notice it was missing until he opened his chest to get the gun for the colonel. But the doctor confirms that's what it was."

"Toxin? For hunting?" Fitz asked. "Sounds like cheating."

"Well, you saw what that gun did," Tassa said. "I'm not sure the captain is interested in giving his quarry a fighting chance."

"Is the doctor still with her?" Fitz asked.

"Yes. He's just making sure she keeps the anti-toxin down before he leaves her. But she's doing fine, so he should be by in a minute," Tassa said.

"Good. The colonel wanted to speak with him," Fitz said.

"I'll let him know," Tassa said, then gave him an awkward little wave before heading back to her own train car.

He turned to walk back to Moreau, who was still waiting outside their cabin door, but stopped before crossing in front of the colonel's door.

He could hear Weld in there, raging. He moved to stand against the wall as close to the door as he could get without being seen. Moreau on the other side did the same. He could see the shock on her face as Weld ranted and realized she really had had no clue. She had been in the cabin studying while the rest of them had been plotting and counter-plotting.

And from the wideness of her eyes and the way she put her hand over her mouth as if to contain her own gasps of alarm, he knew Ritchie was right.

She was going to be so pissed when she worked out that he and Ritchie knew Weld was likely guilty and hadn't told her. He felt bad about that now, even though he was pretty sure she had always been perfectly safe, even alone with Weld.

"Mr. Weld," the colonel said, trying to bring Weld's long rant about the Lady Fabron and all that she had done to his family to some kind of close. When Weld just kept talking over him, he spoke more loudly. "I can have you sedated, Mr. Weld, if it will help."

"What do I care?" Weld snapped. "What do I care about anything now?"

"You care," the colonel said. "Otherwise you would've jumped out of that train car. Or charged at me with your shiny knives and forced me to shoot you."

"I didn't break any laws," Weld said.

"Damage to property," the colonel said.

"To a Felzkinder whose owner is dead?" Weld scoffed. "Who cares?"

"Well, part of your problem is that a lot of people cared about that Felzkinder," the colonel said.

"So many actual people suffering in this universe," Weld said, but then corrected himself. "In this Union of Free Worlds, even. But who cares about that? Someone hurt a Felzkinder."

"Someone also attempted to murder one of my cadets," the colonel said mildly.

"I didn't want to," Weld said. Fitz could feel Moreau's eyes on him, questioning, but he didn't look up at her. She could work it out on her own from here. No, what was tearing at him was the regret in Weld's voice. It sounded so real.

Why should that matter to him? What good did regret do to the world? Fitz had regrets of his own. Some of the biggest ones were also attached to Ritchie. But he couldn't do anything about them. He couldn't make up for what he had done, not even if he tried.

And he was forbidden to try.

He had no sympathy for Weld. None at all.

"Mr. Weld, you will not be getting off the train at the academy," the colonel was saying, and Fitz quieted his own thoughts to listen in once more.

"I assumed I was under military arrest," Weld said.

"No. As serious as attempted murder of a cadet may be, it's not the chiefest of your crimes," the colonel said.

"I don't understand. Lady Fabron died of a heart attack, and the Felzkinder was legally property."

"The train, you fool," the colonel said, finally losing his carefully contained patience. "More than the train, our implants. You spoofed systems that weren't supposed to be spoofable."

"It wasn't hard," Weld said. "I'm in trouble for that?"

"Trouble is putting it far too mildly," the colonel said. "So you'll be riding the train to the end of the line, where you'll be met with representatives from several government organizations. They're going to want to know everything you know, and how and where you learned it. I strongly urge you to be forthright with them. You didn't just work this out watching other maintenance workers on the trains, did you?"

There was a long, tense moment where Fitz listened as intently as he could, until he could practically hear his eardrums humming in frantic search for any sound at all. But there was none.

"Well, as you will," the colonel said. "I'm sealing you in this room now. But think about what I said. But keep in mind, you're going to be working uphill to get these agents you're about to meet to trust you. Because they'll be hearing my report first, and my recommendation to them is to just start with the chemical interrogations and work from there."

Weld sputtered, then made a sound somewhere between a scream and a sob.

Then the colonel was standing in the hall between Moreau and Fitz, calmly shutting his own cabin door. The moment it closed, all sound from within was cut off.

Which was a shame. It sounded like Weld was more than halfway to an apoplexy.

"Chemical interrogation, sir?" Moreau asked in the smallest voice Fitz had ever heard.

"I don't like it either, cadet," he said to her. "But I've looked at Mr. Weld's educational records." He glanced over at Fitz, as if acknowledging he had done this at some point after Ritchie had asked him to. "He shouldn't be able to do what he did. And he has demonstrated a pattern of lying and covering up. He has an affinity for it. Given what's on the line—train line security and possibly more systems than that—we don't have time to mess around."

"Are you saying you think he's a spy?" Moreau asked. "For who?"

"I don't know," the colonel said. "Maybe I'm wrong. Maybe he's just a messed-up kid who figured out some tricks. I hope that's all it is. But if I were one of our many enemies looking for an in at the Union of Free Worlds foreign services, Mr. Weld is just the sort of target I'd exploit."

"A messed-up kid with some tricks," Fitz said. "Ironic."

"Well, it's out of our hands now," the colonel said. "Where is that doctor?"

"Tassa promised to send him here when he's done with Ritchie," Fitz said.

"Hm. Tassa," the colonel said, as if making a mental note. "Well, no reason to wait. Let's go to them."

Moreau took half a step back towards the cabin, but the colonel turned and raised his eyebrows as if surprised at her actions. She seemed stuck between actions, not sure what to do, but when Fitz waved for her to come with them, she ran to fall into step beside him.

"Sorry you got left out of things there," Fitz said to her. "We should've kept you in the loop."

"Well, even out of the loop, I was a team player, wasn't I?" she said as they moved from one sleeper car to the next. "I made a very effective babysitter. To a murderer."

"Yes, you did," Fitz said.

21

IT FELT WEIRD, being in a VIP car. There was so much room to move around, and she could see out the windows without even getting out of the spacious bed.

Not that Ritchie had gotten to look out of the windows much. Whatever that doctor had given her, or more likely whatever Weld had given her, was making the world wash in and out, and she didn't always catch the distinctions between awake and asleep.

She remembered the colonel being there, and Fitz, and even Moreau. But mostly she remembered how soft the blankets were, how cool the pillow under her cheek, how the gentle rocking of the train made her feel like she was in a giant cradle.

But when the train started to slow to a stop, and that rocking faded away, she was instantly awake and alert. She threw back the covers and ran to the window to see where they were.

They were in a high alpine meadow, flat and treeless. The rain had finally eased off and shafts of watery sunlight were penetrating through the cloud cover, highlighting this tuft of grass or that nodding bed of flowers.

"This must be Lady Fabron's estate," Fitz said, yawing as he unfolded himself from the easy chair he had been sleeping in. She hadn't even realized he was there.

"It's huge," Ritchie said, looking at the imposing structure just rolling into view. "All of that just for her?"

"Well, not just for her," said a voice from the doorway and Ritchie turned to see Baptiste Rose standing in the corridor, a collection of small bags flung over his shoulders or tucked under his arms.

"You live there too, of course," Ritchie said.

"Not just me," he said. "May I come in?"

"Of course," Ritchie said, waving for him to join her at the window.

"There's a staff of about ten of us who live and work there full time," he said as he looked out at the building. "And nearly a hundred Felzkinders."

"A hundred!" Ritchie gasped. "She had so many?"

"My lady rescued so many," he gently corrected her. "Some were abandoned. Some were declared sentient but found living on their own too difficult. Most of them are older models; the younger ones are thriving on their own better."

"And you take care of them all?" Ritchie asked.

"My lady did," he said. "It's all on me now. Which is why I had to come and see you before I disembarked from the train. I had to thank you."

"Thank me? For what?" Ritchie asked.

"For pushing your investigation," he said. "I was willing to believe, well, anything if it made it all go away. What I didn't understand was that the lawyers were prepared to blame me. Negligence of care, some such thing. They meant to wrestle control of the estate away from me and the others who work here. It would've been the death of all of our Felzkinders."

"That sounds evil," Ritchie said.

Mr. Rose shrugged. "I'm sure on paper, this all looks like a waste of money. A bad way to preserve a fortune. But my lady didn't want to preserve that fortune. She wanted to use it all to save every creature like her beloved Chou-Chou. But they only look at the numbers, because that's their job."

"But it's safe now? The money?" Fitz asked.

"Yes, thanks to the two of you," he said. "I let my grief overwhelm me, and I almost lost everything. You have my undying gratitude. Please forgive any cross words I may have directed towards you before. I owe you everything. Thank you for pushing for the truth."

"I did it for Chou-Chou," Ritchie said.

"What will you do now?" Fitz asked. The train had come to a complete halt and Mr. Rose gathered up his bags once more.

"Well, the first step will to be reconsidering the estate's legal representation," he said. "Then, I shall devote the rest of my days to carrying on my lady's final mission."

Fitz shot Ritchie a glance she ignored as she gave Mr. Rose her brightest smile. "Best of luck to you," she said.

"And best of luck to you too at your new academy," he said. Then, with a little bow, he was gone.

The moment he was well out of earshot, Fitz let out a scoff.

"What?" Ritchie asked.

"Well, I'm sure it's good work, and I admire him for doing it," Fitz said. "But Weld isn't wrong about the Lady Fabron being party to war crimes. If she thought that cleared her ledger, I'd have to say she still came up far short in the 'good things' column."

"Maybe," Ritchie said. "But I don't think she saw it that way. I think she really did just want to save other creatures like Chou-Chou because she loved Chou-Chou."

"And that's noble?"

"I don't know. I don't think things balance out like that," she said. "But I don't think the Lady Fabron thought about it like that either. Because in her head, nothing she did was a crime. She was always acting correctly. From her point of view. She could never make up for it until she admitted she had done wrong, and she died never having come to that realization at all. I don't see any justice in this whole thing, not from any angle."

She dropped back down on the edge of the bed, suddenly tired again. How much had she slept? It felt like days. It felt like minutes.

"Weld will be held accountable," Fitz said.

"Not for Chou-Chou," Ritchie said.

"For a lot of other stuff that might end up being a lot more important," Fitz said. "No offense to Chou-Chou."

Ritchie shrugged, then sighed. "I get what you're saying," she said. "And on one level, I agree. On another, I can't help thinking there must have been some way to save Weld. Not the three of us; we met him far too late. But if Lady Fabron and her people had never done what they did, what might have become of Weld?"

"He might have been better, but he might have been worse," Fitz said. "We have no way of knowing. And you are going to drive yourself mad trying to figure it out. It's unknowable. Let it go."

Ritchie nodded, but said nothing.

The train started moving again. They both looked out through the window to see Mr. Rose standing alone on the train platform, a small mountain of chests and crates around him.

Including a crate large enough to contain the Lady Fabron. And beside it, a smaller one for Chou-Chou.

"How much longer until we get to the academy?" Ritchie asked.

"Not long now," Fitz said. "Not long at all."

22

CAPTAIN BERGER WAS the second passenger to be dropped off, not far from the Lady Fabron's estate. He disembarked without feeling he owed anything at all to Fitz or Ritchie, no apologies for his own cross words or anything.

Perhaps he felt the loan of his gun had evened up everything. Fitz didn't feel like it had, but then again, he didn't really want to have another conversation with the captain, either.

Ritchie had gone back to sleep, and Moreau was once more studying alone in their cabin. Earlier in the trip, he had assumed she was only holding the reader while she daydreamed about parties past and parties future. Now he was beginning to suspect she really was studying that hard.

He just hoped she warmed to Ritchie, because the two were pretty much guaranteed to be roommates. And Fitz would be on his own until another even more last-minute recruit was found.

Fitz went to the observation car to watch for the first glimpse of the academy grounds. The train was no longer snaking through the valleys and canyons but was climbing around and around one of the taller peaks, so he settled into one of the chairs and let it tilt back beneath him so he could watch the peak above.

The school was on the top, built into the mountain. He wasn't sure what he would be able to see from the train. He was expecting something gloomier than the Lady Fabron's estate, and that had been pretty morose.

It was going to be a long three years.

"Cadet Fitz," Feliks said from the doorway. "There's a holo call for you."

He sounded like he couldn't even believe the words coming out of his own mouth. Fitz couldn't blame him. Holo calls involved sending and receiving enormous amounts of data. Expensive when sent locally; astronomically expensive when broadcast through jump space.

And he knew this wasn't a local call.

"I can take it here," Fitz said, getting up from his chair.

"I'll send it through," Feliks said, already on his way back out the door.

Fitz smoothed down the front of his tunic, then gave his hair a hard tousle. If anyone had ever asked, he would not be able to say why it was so important to him that one part of his appearance be neat and the other to absolutely not be. He just knew the combination was always guaranteed to irritate his father.

"Father," he said as the hologram flickered to life in front of him, quite spoiling his view of the mountain.

"Did we not agree on the importance of keeping a low profile?" General Shackleton Fitz III demanded.

"How am I not keeping a low profile?" Fitz asked. Surely after everything that happened, the colonel hadn't sent any sort of disciplinary message about him ahead to the academy? Because Fitz had broken some rules, but he thought the colonel agreed they were in the service of a greater good.

But what else could be making his father's forehead go so purple and bulgy?

"Your name is turning up on scads of reports," his father said, throwing his hands out as if Fitz could see those reports displaying on the desktop in front of him. He couldn't. The hologram never included the desk. Fitz's lack of security clearance made that impossible.

"Reports from a dozen agencies. Law enforcement, intelligence, security systems."

"Oh, that," Fitz said with a dismissive wave his father didn't like at all. "But wait. Did you read the reports or just see my name?"

"I don't care what you did. I don't care why you did it," his father said in his low, rumbling voice. Which meant that he had read those reports. "We agreed you would keep a low profile. Not attract attention. This!" he jabbed his fingers down at his desk. "Is attention!"

"Sorry, sir," Fitz said. He could feel the train beneath him begin to slow. They were finally approaching the academy, although he could see nothing from around his father. "Things got out of hand. I should've done things differently. It won't happen again."

"I wished I could believe that, son," his father said with a sigh.

"I meant it when I promised I'd do well here," Fitz said. His father's eyebrows went up.

"Oh, that was a promise to me, was it? When you said it, it sounded more like a threat."

"Well, I was angry at the time," Fitz said. "But what does it matter? I meant what I said."

"You always mean what you say," his father said, and Fitz fought the urge to laugh in his hologram face. That was so very far from the truth, and they both knew it. But his father's expression was still deadly serious, and Fitz realized with a sinking feeling that his name on all of those reports about the capture of the criminal and possible spy Cadmar Weld wasn't the real reason for his father's call.

"Father," he said, but his father cut him off.

"I know she's there with you," he said. "I would never have agreed for you to go there, if I'd known before."

"Yes, you would've," Fitz said, the words out before he could take them back. "It was this or nothing. No, the thing you never would've done was allow her to be here."

"You're right," his father said. "I thought my instructions had been clear on that matter, but someone let something slip through. She shouldn't be there, not with you or without you there. But it's too late to change things now."

"Because her name is on all of those reports, too," Fitz guessed. "Bigger than mine, I'm sure. More frequently mentioned."

"It doesn't matter," his father said. "It doesn't change anything. I don't like the fact that she's there. I don't like testing you in this way. You're not good at tests."

"Oh, really?" Fitz asked. "Because the only test that ever counted, the 'can Fitz keep his big fat mouth shut' test? I've been passing that over and over again for years now."

"Don't fail it now," his father said. "This affects more than you and me now."

"I know, father," Fitz said. "I swore I wouldn't say a word. I won't say a word."

"Not even to her?" his father asked.

Fitz closed his eyes and took a deep breath. Then he opened them and looked straight into the hologram simulation of his father's eyes. Somewhere in another entire quadrant, a hologram of him stood in his father's office doing the same.

"Not even to her," he swore. The train came to a complete halt, and his father noticed as he compensated for the lurch. "I have to go. We're there now."

"Go," he said, and then his hologram was gone. No best of luck, no words of affection.

Fitz walked back through the train one last time to fetch his bag then disembark. As he came into their sleeper car, he saw Ritchie there with Moreau, waiting for him so they could all go out onto the platform together. She gave him a nervous smile.

What did it matter anyway, the secret he was keeping from her? She seemed to have done just fine, not knowing what really happened that day. She was adjusting. She had even somehow defeated his father's attempts to steer her fate away from the foreign service.

But it did matter. Because they could never truly be friends again, not like they had been before. And that friendship had been everything to him. The years in between, the years without her, had only made him realize just how rare and wonderful their friendship had been.

But it was gone forever. And only one of them knew it.

23

COLONEL HANSEN WAS ALREADY WAITING on the train platform when the three of them stepped down. Ritchie looked all around, but there was no sign of a school anywhere. Just the jagged side of a mountain wreathed in wisps of gray clouds.

"Where is it?" Ritchie asked.

"Someone is coming to meet us once the train departs," the colonel told her. "How are you feeling?"

"Tip-top," she lied. She wanted a dozen more naps before facing this next challenge, but she'd muddle through somehow.

"I don't know why you're nervous," Moreau said to her. "You get to start out already famous. That's got to be worth a lot."

"I didn't ask to be famous," Ritchie said, running her thumb over the name tag on her uniform.

"I didn't mean that," Moreau said, looking genuinely chagrined. "I meant about what happened on the train. With Weld."

"But why would anyone know about that?" Ritchie asked.

"It's a news story," Fitz said. "I've already heard from my father on account of it. The universe at large might not notice it, but in the world of foreign service, you've just made quite a little name for yourself."

"Oh," Ritchie said. She hadn't realized any of that was even a possibility. She had just wanted to be sure that Chou-Chou's murderer didn't get away with it.

Was this going to be a good thing or a bad thing?

"Cadets," the colonel said so suddenly they all snapped to attention. "I've been summoned to the administrative offices. You three are to wait here until your escort comes down. They'll give you the tour and get you settled."

"Yes, sir," they said. The train was just pulling away from the platform behind them, and they watched as the figure of Colonel Hansen slowly disappeared among the blowing strands of cloud.

There was no bench to sit on, so the three of them just wandered around the platform as the train turned the corner of the mountain and was gone. Then the silence was absolute. No birds twittered, no insects hummed. There was just the sound of wind through the short grass, barely louder than a sigh.

"Here we go," Fitz said, and Ritchie saw two figures coming down the mountain towards the platform. There didn't seem to be any sort of path for them to follow, and yet they picked their way around fields of loose rock and through tall tufts of meadow grass, as if they knew a particular way.

They were wearing cloaks and thick furry hats, so it wasn't until they were quite close that it was apparent that one was a boy and the other a girl. Their expressions were stoic, but when the boy looked at each of them, there was a friendly gleam to his eye.

Not so with the girl.

"Moreau, Fitz, Ritchie," she said, and they snapped to attention all in a line. She looked them over, the twist of her lips telling them clearly she was not pleased with what she saw.

"Is that hair regulation?" she asked Moreau.

"It is within guidelines, yes," Moreau said.

"Well, we'll be checking that for sure," the girl said and moved over to look at Fitz. "I know you," she said to him.

"Do you?" he said, glancing down at her name tag. Ritchie risked a glance over at it herself. JEGER.

"You washed out of my first school, Roma 5," Jeger said. "You washed out quite quickly. And yet you're here."

"With you," Fitz said. Jeger scowled.

"I was moved here because there was a lack of skilled upper classmen to guide the others," she said. "For me, it's an honor to be here. For you, maybe not so much."

Fitz said nothing, but Ritchie could practically hear him biting down on his tongue, holding back a plethora of sarcastic responses.

Maybe he really was growing.

Ritchie straightened her spine as Jeger moved to stand in front of her. "Ritchie," she said, ostentatiously reading it off her uniform, although clearly she had known it when she said it before. "I know that name."

Ritchie said nothing. She was far too used to this.

Jeger turned to the other cadet, whose name tag read BALE. "I know that name. Where do I know that name?"

"She's a new recruit, not a transplant," Bale told her.

"True enough," Jeger said, looking at Ritchie again. "Wait a minute, I know where I know that name. That ambassador, the one taken by the Yuffids. His name was Ritchie."

"*Is* Ritchie," Ritchie said. "He's not dead."

"Not so far as we know," Jeger said drily. "Still, a bit of a cockup that was, wasn't it? And now you want to join the foreign service too? I guess we can just hope you're a bit more on top of things than your father."

Then, to Ritchie's surprise, Moreau spoke up before she could muster up a response. "That's ancient history," Moreau said. "And if you've been keeping up with more current events, you'd know it's not even relevant. Ritchie has done more to prove her value on the ride here than you've done in the nearly four years you've been a cadet."

"She's not wrong," Fitz added. "You want to bust Ritchie's chops, bust *her* chops. She can take it. But leave her father out of it."

"Is that a threat, cadet?" Jeger demanded, turning her full glower on Fitz, who met it without backing down.

"If it needs to be," he said.

"Storm's coming," Bale said. Jeger spun to shoot a glare at him, but he just pointed to dark clouds flowing in between their mountain peak and the next one to their south. "Hey, I don't want to walk through that if we don't have to. Plenty of time to break these three when we get up there."

Jeger turned to stare the three of them down one more time. Then she held up a single finger. "Don't cross me. I can end your careers with a word. Now fall in."

Rain was starting to fall before they even stepped off the platform, and without the cloaks that Jeger and Bale were wearing, the other three were quickly soaked through.

And they had no idea how far they had to climb to get to the academy. All that could be seen ahead of them was rock and rain.

Ritchie clutched her bag a bit higher on her shoulder and concentrated on putting one foot in front of the other.

That, and not dwelling on how close to the truth Jeger had just come with what was probably only a random stab. Most people who figured out who Ritchie was, and who her father was, the knowledge made them feel sorry for Ritchie.

She hated that pity. Because she didn't deserve it.

The big cockup that had gotten her father taken hostage by a race of aliens no one in the Union of Free Worlds still could understand?

It had been hers.

CHECK OUT BOOK TWO!

The Ritchie and Fitz Sci-Fi Murder Mysteries continue with book two, Murder in the Skies.

Murdina Ritchie put everything on the line to earn one chance to prove herself at the Oymyakon Foreign Service Academy. Just one chance. Despite the bad reputation that comes with her family name, despite the bullies desperate to see her fail, she refuses to back down from any opportunity to show her worth.

Everyone at the academy knows her skill, knows her inability to compromise in the pursuit of excellence, and knows her drive for success at all costs that borders on desperation.

But all of that common knowledge works against her when a bullying upper class cadet dies in a freak training accident that looks a lot like murder. Because now everyone knows that Murdina Ritchie tops any possible list of suspects.

Suddenly she finds a goal beyond proving her worth: proving her own innocence.

Murder in the Skies, the second book in the Ritchie and Fitz Sci-Fi Murder Mystery series. Check it out!

NEW SERIES: THE FORGOTTEN PLANET

Coming soon from Ratatoskr Press Books, the new YA sci-fi series *The Forgotten Planet* starts with book 1: *Raiding the Forgotten Derelict*.

History sleeps beneath them all, but only she sees it.

Lafayette Eloi always knew her parents thought differently from others. They kept their books buried beneath her mother's house. They spoke an old language in the dead of night, whispering behind closed doors and bolted shutters. She grew up in a village where no one was related to her, and she never knew why.

Then, after her mother died, her father came to fetch her. Now she and her mother's dog assist her father in his work. The work discussed in whispers in the dark. The work that had cost Lafayette so much all her young life.

But now she learns just how much her father's work means to their entire world. Only no one knows anything about it. Only her father. And only Lafayette.

Because the work that consumed her father's entire life and her mother's too now nibbles at the fringe's of Lafayette's own life. And she cannot refuse its call.

Raiding the Forgotten Derelict, first book in the new YA sci-fu series *The Forgotten Planet,* available in September 2024 from Ratatoskr Press Books.

COMPLETE SERIES: THE RITCHIE AND FITZ SCI-FI MURDER MYSTERIES

The Ritchie and Fitz Sci-Fi Murder Mysteries starts with *Murder on the Intergalactic Railway*.

For Murdina Ritchie, acceptance at the Oymyakon Foreign Service Academy means one last chance at her dream of becoming a diplomat for the Union of Free Worlds. For Shackleton Fitz IV, it represents his last chance not to fail out of military service entirely.

Strange that fate should throw them together now, among the last group of students admitted after the start of the semester. They had once shared the strongest of friendships. But that all ended a long time ago.

But when an insufferable but politically important woman turns up murdered, the two agree to put their differences aside and work together to solve the case.

Because the murderer might strike again. But more importantly, solving a murder would just have to impress the dour colonel who clearly thinks neither of them belong at his academy.

Murder on the Intergalactic Railway, the first book in *The Ritchie and Fitz Sci-Fi Murder Mysteries.*

COMPLETE SERIES: THE TRAVELS OF SCOUT SHANNON

The complete six-book series *The Travels of Scout Shannon* begin with book one, *Under Falling Skies*.

Scout Shannon's whole family died the day the Space Farers dropped an asteroid on their domed city. Now she lives alone, out in the wild with only her dogs for company. She prefers it that way.

But Scout finds herself at a crossroads. One road leads back to a quiet life snug under the protective dome of a city. The other road leads to a life in the rebellion, a life of adventure and excitement but also danger. Dare she try to find the rebels hiding in the hills?

Then a chance encounter with a stranger from the other side of the galaxy threatens to derail what remains of Scout's life. The entire galaxy awaits her, if she survives the next four days.

Under Falling Skies, a young adult science fiction novel, set on a remote planet with a distinctly Old West feel. For fans of gunslinging women and young girl assassins. And dogs.

Under Falling Skies, the first book in *The Travels of Scout Shannon,* available everywhere now.

SCI-FI SERIAL PODCAST!

Check out my new monthly podcast of serialized science fiction: THE TALES OF THE CHAI MAKHANI TRIO!

Elyot loathes the massive Commonwealth ships that hover menacingly over his home world of Adghal. He hates the Commonwealth enforcers who harass the populace even more. But with his mother missing and presumed dead, Elyot keeps his head down and strives to avoid notice. And he succeeds until the day two strangers enter his life...

New episodes of this sci-fi serial drop every 1st of the month.

Now streaming on all major podcast platforms. Also available in eBook and print everywhere books or sold. For a complete episode listing, check out the page on my website.

ALSO FROM KATE MACLEOD

Love heists and capers? Then check out my new series, *The Vic Harper Capers*. The action starts with the novella THE THIRD POLE JOB.

Vic Harper and her gang retired wealthy from their life of thievery and heists. Whether in a luxury condo overlooking the river in Minneapolis or in a modernist mansion built into the side of a mountain in Colorado, life comes easy now.

Perhaps too easy.

When an old friend asks for a favor his niece, Vic and her mentor Chase Woodward leap at the chance to relieve a little of the boredom. But a quick bit of B&E in a wealthy suburb of Chicago leads to an even greater challenge.

The prize? Nothing much. Just the opportunity to level a playing field for their friend's niece.

But the heist? May prove to be their toughest ever. Because to get to the prize, they'll have to climb a mountain.

And not just any mountain. Their prize waits on the summit of Mount Everest.

THE THIRD POLE JOB, the first novella in *The Vic Harper Capers*. For those who love capers, heists and other impossible missions.

ALSO FROM RATATOSKR PRESS

Also from Ratatoskr Press, *The Witches Three Cozy Mystery Series* by Cate Martin, a mix of mystery and magic that begins with Book 1: *Charm School*.

Amanda Clarke thinks of herself as perfectly ordinary in every way. Just a small-town girl who serves breakfast all day in a little diner nestled next to the highway, nothing but dairy farms for miles around. She fits in there.

But then an old woman she never met dies, and Amanda was named in her will. Now Amanda packs a bag and heads to the big city, to Miss Zenobia Weekes' Charm School for Exceptional Young Ladies. And it's not in just any neighborhood. No, she finds herself on Summit Avenue in St. Paul, a street lined with gorgeous old houses, the former homes of lumber barons, railroad millionaires, even the writer F. Scott Fitzgerald. Why, Amanda can practically hear the jazz music still playing across the decades.

Scratch that. The music really, literally, still plays in the backyard of the charm school. Because the house stretches across time itself. Without a witch to protect this tear in the fabric of the world, anything can spill over. Like music.

Or like murder.

The complete series is out now, and it all starts with *Charm School*.

FREE EBOOK!

Like exclusive, free content?

To get two prequel short stories to THE RITCHIE AND FITZ SCI-FI MURDER MYSTERIES as well as a bonus prequel novelette to the completed six-book series THE TRAVELS OF SCOUT SHANNON, signup for my monthly newsletter at KateMacLeodWrites.com.

Thank you!

ABOUT THE AUTHOR

Photograph © 2016 Jonathan Conklin

Kate MacLeod has written stories which have appeared in *Analog*, *Strange Horizons* and *Mythic Delirium*, among other places. She is also the author of two young adult science fictions series: *The Travels of Scout Shannon*, and *The Ritchie and Fitz Sci-Fi Murder Mysteries*. She also contributes to a serialized science fiction podcast called *The Tales of the Chai Makhani Trio*. She currently lives in Minneapolis, Minnesota.

Find out more about the author and sign up for her newsletter at KateMacLeodWrites.com.

ALSO BY KATE MACLEOD

Novels

The Slums of the Solar System:

Mitwa

The Mars of Malcontents

The Whole World for Each

Books 1-3 Box Set

The Travels of Scout Shannon:

Under Falling Skies

In Quaking Hills

Among Treacherous Stars

Against Impassable Barriers

Over Freezing Altitudes

At Galactic Central

The Travels of Scout Shannon Books 1-3

The Travels of Scout Shannon Books 4-6

The Travels of Scout Shannon Books 1-6

The Ritchie and Fitz Sci-Fi Murder Mysteries:

Murder on the Intergalactic Railway

Murder in the Skies

Body in the Catacombs

Death on the Summit

An Undiplomatic Murder

A Lethal Betrayal

The Forgotten Planet

Raiding the Forgotten Derelict (Forthcoming September 2024)

Sci-Fi Novellas

The Intergenerational Tree

I Rise into a Daybreak

Caper Novellas

The Third Pole Job

The Twelve Days of Christmas Job

10-Story Collections

Tales of Blood and Ink

Tales of Old Gods and New

5-Story Collections

Tales from Heian-Kyo and Others

Tales from the Edges and Ends

Tales from Forgotten Days

Tales from Ancient and Future Times

Tales from Across Space